PLASTIC JESUS

AND OTHER STORIES

PLASTIC JESUS

AND OTHER STORIES

JUDITH ETS-HOKIN

atmosphere press

austin, tx

For Margaret and Carl

Life imitates Art far more than
Art imitates Life.

- Oscar Wilde

CONTENTS

PREFACE

I began making up stories when I was five or six, stories about all kinds of things, marriage, kids, my relatives...and they were harmless, child make-believe.

Today, my made-up stories, are called *fiction.*

So finally, I have a collection of stories, beginning with *Plastic Jesus,* the germ of which began when I first heard the song on the radio in 1962.

The other stories in the collection were written at various times, some quite recently. After enjoying a long business life, I have now come home, where I am spending my time
writing,
writing,
and writing.

PLASTIC JESUS, PART 1

I am bought by a lady. I feel her soft hands pick me up and soon I am looking directly into her pale blue eyes. Her skin is fair and wrinkled and her gray hair is pulled back from her face. We stare at each other and then she says,

"Sweet Jesus, my name is Violet, and you're coming home with me."

Inside the gray sedan, I hear her peel the cellophane from the stick-um at the base of my stand and watch as she fastens it firmly in place in the center of the dashboard. Putting me back on my stand, she says softly,

"This is your new home, little Jesus." She gestures toward the windshield and beyond, and says, "From here, you'll be able to see the world."

When I was living on a glass shelf with rows of my replicas, a price sticker pasted on my back, I had no idea what my life was going to be like; now I feel blessed.

I feel the warmth of the sun coming through the windshield as we drive out of the parking lot and onto the street. I see sidewalks and buildings and people. It's all so interesting; I can't wait to see the rest of the world.

As it turns out, the world I usually see is on Tuesday and Friday mornings when Violet and I go shopping. On these twice-weekly excursions, I hear the car door open, I hear Violet climb in, and I feel her soft hands pick me up and turn me to face her. I look directly into her pale blue eyes and each time I see a great sadness in them. For some reason, it gives me a strong tingly feeling; somehow, and in some way, I want to make her feel better.

Violet is a small woman and her figure is slender and compact. She dresses nicely, in long-sleeved shifts, or sometimes in a black sweater and slim skirt, with a coat and a small, dark-colored hat perched a bit sideways on her head. She never fails to greet me.

"Hello, Sweet Jesus, it makes me so happy just to see you," she often says, then places me back on my stand before starting the car and backing it out of the garage. Once on the road, she talks to me non-stop as we travel the familiar streets to the grocery store.

"Sweet Jesus," she'll say, "my dear friend Nellie called me this morning to tell me her nephew is visiting, and invited me to join them for dinner," or...

"Oh, how I wish my Bobby was well enough to come for dinner," or...

"Sweet Jesus, I've never told anyone this but I feel so regretful for never having married," or...

"Mother always told me I was too good for any of the men I liked and then time went so fast," or...

"Sweet Jesus, it shames me to confess that I used to pretend the children in my classes were my own, and imagined taking them home with me," and so on, talking about her life until we pull into a parking lot filled with cars.

Then she gets out of the car and leaves me alone to gaze at all the people coming and going with bags of groceries, kids playing and running alongside their parents. Seeing all this makes me want to talk and walk along with them, and I get that same tingly feeling in my plastic body as when I look into Violet's sad eyes. Surely, I have something to give to Violet and to all these others.

In addition to our Tuesday and Friday shopping trips, on Sundays we drive out to the country and park on a little knoll overlooking large gardens and a big rambling brick building that has iron bars on the second and third-floor windows. There is a sign painted in black letters over the double front doors: Pinewood Sanitarium. Violet lifts me off my base and looks into my eyes as she makes the sign of a cross, moving her other hand up and down and across her breast, and murmurs,

"Sweet Lord Jesus, twenty-four years ago I asked you for a

child, and you gave me Bobby. I have not asked for anything sincse. Now, I ask only that you make him well."

Then, seemingly exhausted, she sits quietly, her head bowed. Clutching me in her hand, she stares at me, as if expecting me to say something. But what would I say? What could I say? Again, I feel that tingly sensation.

After a time, Violet puts me back on my base, gets out of the car, and disappears into the sanitarium.

While I wait for her, I watch the activity outside: people sitting on benches and walking along the gravel paths that loop through flower gardens in bloom. Sometimes Violet returns alone and other times with an unhappy-looking young man of about twenty-five with pale hair and eyes. His name is Bobby.

On those days, the three of us go to a drive-thru restaurant. Bobby always orders the same thing: a double burger with French fries and a chocolate milkshake. Sometimes he asks to go to the zoo, and I like that because I enjoy seeing children getting in and out of cars while I wait in the parking lot.

It is not as interesting when we go to the movies because then we park in a dark garage and there are no people for me to watch. People are fascinating to me because they are all so different: blonde hair, black hair, tall, short, thin, fat, and all of them makes me feel that perhaps I have something for them, though I have no idea what. As for Bobby, he is sullen and quiet most of the time. He calls Violet "Auntie."

"Auntie Violet," he says, "when are you going to let me come home?"

"When you are well," she says, "then we can do all the things you like to do." He doesn't reply.

One day when the three of us are out driving, Violet parks the car in front of a group of shops and disappears inside one of them. Suddenly, I feel Bobby's cold hand encircle my body. He lifts me up and brings me close to his face. His large, pale blue eyes stare at me for a moment.

"Isn't there anything you can do to get rid of Violet?" he asks me. "If she wasn't around, they couldn't keep me in that nut house. Come on, you're supposed to help people."

He holds me so long and so tight that my body vibrates and I feel like I might explode. I am relieved when Violet returns to the car and he places me back on my stand. Bobby frightens me, and I am not used to angry feelings. Besides, I wonder why he feels that way since Violet is always so nice.

Then, one Tuesday, Violet does not come. I wait. I wait and wait and wait. Days later, the garage doors swing open, and two strange men appear in front of me, and I see the day is very bright and sunny.

"See if she will start," one of the men says. "I don't think she's been driven since the old lady croaked. If you can't get her started, we'll tow her to the yard."

END PART 1

CHANCE

Kathy knew the rules before they began. Call on his secret cell, the one only she knew about. Always sound impersonal and business-like if anyone was around. No perfume or lipstick on the days they made love. No babies. (She'd had her tubes tied, though it didn't matter now as she was past child bearing.)

It had been nearly fifteen years and Charles had promised that tonight he finally would tell his wife he was leaving. They had to wait until after he received the prestigious National Integrity Award, a highly regarded event organized to commemorate the United Nations International Anti-Corruption Day. Those receiving this award were individuals who had worked to eradicate corruption and establish good governance in maintaining the highest standards of business. A thousand-dollar testimonial dinner benefiting The American Heart Association was taking place. Kathy was at home waiting for Charles to call her after the dinner and after he had told his wife he was leaving.

The plan was to meet at the airport. He had told her there would be a limo waiting because he wanted her to ride in style. As his secretary, she had made all the other arrangements and now, finally, waited for the phone to ring. It was 10:30; why hadn't he called? At 11:15 she called his private cell.

"Have you told her?"

"Not yet. We're still here at the testimonial."

"Okay," Kathy said, and for the first time added, "If you don't, I will."

There was a long silence.

"Okay, okay." Charles said. "I'll call you back."

At 1:30 AM Charles called. "It's done; the car is waiting for you, darling."

Finally, Kathy felt ebullient and aware of her heart beating. Excited and a little scared but filled with cheerful expectation, she grabbed her bag and walked out of the apartment. She took the elevator down, walked out the entrance of her building, and saw the car waiting.

The driver nodded as he held the door for her. She stepped in and sank into the soft leather upholstery as the car smoothly and quietly took off. Kathy could see the headlights coming toward them in the dark and then felt the thunderous, violent collision. The last impression Kathy had was the explosion of light that seemed to appear all around her.

Charles arrived at the airport still trying to reach Kathy on their secret cell. He felt annoyed when again there was no answer.

"Dammit Kathy, I've finally told my wife and went through a terrible scene with her to meet you here to start the new life you're always talking about and now you won't answer your goddamned phone."

EDWARD AND STELLA

Shuddering and spewing fumes, the silver-and-red bus pulled to a stop immediately in front of Edward. The bus waited as he grasped the shiny metal railing and braced himself for the first long step up.

"Let me help you, sir," said a young, slender, blond girl with a backpack, standing behind him.

Edward gripped the bar and, aided by the girl's strength, managed the first step. The next one was not difficult. He nodded and thanked her; she smiled, dropped her fare into the box, and bounced down the narrow aisle. *Ah, youth,* he thought, acutely aware of the fact that he had recently celebrated his eightieth year.

He just had time to grab hold of a pole as the bus took off with a roar, the force throwing him from one side to the other. Edward waited a moment to regain his balance, dropped his fare into the box, and then slowly lowered himself into the nearest seat, feeling exhilarated as the bus thundered to the next corner.

He had decided on a whim to do something he had not done in years: to take a ride on a bus. He was a successful attorney and could easily afford a taxi or even a private car and driver. But he wanted to turn back the clock and do something new. And now, he was enjoying the bouncy feeling of the bus as it drove on, stopping at each corner and then taking off with a lurch.

It was a warm June afternoon, and he was alone except for the somber-faced driver and the young girl now seated in the back of the bus, backpack on her lap, engrossed in her book, her blond hair falling forward, nearly covering her face.

Edward's heart quickened, remembering Stella, blond curls tumbling over her face as she bent forward, intent upon her embroidery. His mind slipped back some sixty years.

A large, luxurious 1885 summer residence, the rambling resort hotel, with stained glass, and ornate inlaid wood floors, was painted white. There were forty guest rooms, all with private baths as well as twenty individual cottages. His parents, Greek emigrants, managed the resort where Stella and her family spent the summers. He had been a young man of twenty and she just a little younger. From their first meeting, when she smiled at him and thanked him for helping her with her bag, he knew he loved her but felt intimidated by her family's wealth and social position.

Stella's father was a banker. Edward remembered him clearly. Tall, robust, and domineering, with a large, handlebar mustache. Her mother was small and haughty, a ruffled, bejeweled lady who traveled with two steamer trunks and a personal maid.

Despite this, he still found their daughter enchanting. He leaned his head back against the seat of the bus and closed his eyes, thinking of Stella. He remembered her blond curls and large blue eyes rimmed with dark lashes. Her small straight nose, full lips, fair skin, and slender figure had never left his mind. She'd gone to the most expensive private Eastern schools.

She dressed in the latest Paris fashions and, though often carefree, could be restrained and elegant. Edward saw that she always had young men hovering about her, competing for her attention.

One day, out on a ride, only the two of them, Stella's horse stumbled and came up lame, and Edward invited her to ride home behind him. He could still remember her delicate hands clasped about his waist, her breasts pressed against his back. It was on this ride back that he realized he would ask her to marry him.

For weeks he rehearsed how he would tell her that he loved her, but did not find the courage to say it until nearly the end of summer when he felt desperate at the thought of never seeing her again.

It was a gentle, warm evening with a full moon and a sky filled with stars shimmering on the lake. There was a swing band playing on the open wooden pavilion across the lawn, and Edward remembered his joy when she had accepted his invitation to dance.

They danced and then he asked her if she would sit with him. His heart raced, his legs trembled. His palms had now become sweaty so he didn't dare hold her hand. Edward had prepared a marriage proposal, but found his mouth so dry he couldn't speak.

"Why are you so nervous?" Stella laughed. "Your face looks white!"

He stared at her. The pink paper lanterns covering the strings of lights gave her face a rosy glow. Her hair was iridescent and her eyes shone.

"I want to ask you to marry me," he uttered.

She turned serious then.

"Oh dear, I had no idea," she hesitated. "I didn't know you felt that way." Her face flushed a deep pink.

And then not realizing, he was sure, of the effect her words would have on him, she told him that marriage was impossible. She looked at the dancers whirling about and then back at him.

"Papa would never approve. He has great expectations for me. And your parents are immigrants."

He could only nod, as he understood what she was saying. Edward looked at her with a stiff smile. He felt his life ebbing.

The remembered pain brought him back to the present. He opened his eyes and saw the blond girl; they were still the only passengers on the bus. The air was very warm, stale and close. He took off his dark blue blazer and laid it across his lap. He turned stiffly and, with great effort, managed to open the large heavy window next to him a couple of inches. A warm draft of air refreshed him. He sat back and felt his body begin to relax. His eyes closed again.

After that summer, he had gone back to college and then on to law school where he graduated with honors. He was recruited before he even passed the bar by a large influential firm in New

York, where he became an associate, working sixty to seventy hours a week.

Before he was thirty, he returned to Madison, his hometown, and joined a small, prestigious law firm. Two years later, he married the daughter of one of the partners. Then, shortly after he married, fourteen years since their last dance, he saw Stella again.

He and his wife Jean had gone down to the pier in Madison to see her parents off on a cruise. His wife grabbed his hand and pulled him through the crowd.

"Edward, let's go in front of everyone so Mother and Daddy can see us!"

As they stood on the dock waving goodbye, he recognized Stella, standing on the deck of the ship, her face more beautiful than he had remembered, smiling, talking, animated, leaning affectionately toward the man beside her.

Standing next to his bride, the feelings for Stella he thought were forgotten returned; his heart pounding, he stared at Stella as the cruise ship pulled out of the dock.

He never saw her again after that.

The years flew by. He and Jean had three sons. He became a partner in his father-in-law's firm. The boys grew up and became lawyers, married, and had children of their own. He and Jean had friends and parties and anniversaries. Whenever he thought about his marriage he told himself it was good, but someplace deep inside he knew it was second best. Then, one by one, his friends and acquaintances of many years began passing away. Jean died after a long battle with cancer and Edward believed that his own life was at best in the last quarter.

Nothing seemed to interest or please him anymore. He roamed through his large fine house and garden. He maintained an office at his firm but realized the practice of law no longer held his interest.

"Hey, Dad," his sons would say to him when he came into the office, "what are you doing here on this beautiful day? You should be out on the golf course, enjoying this great weather..."

He felt his sons did not really want him there; the firm was theirs now. He went to his club and played bridge, he played golf, he had dinner in his children's homes, he spent time with his grandchildren, and he worked in his garden, which in the past had brought him such pleasure.

But now, he sometimes felt disoriented, restless, fidgety. And a peculiar thing was happening. Stella had begun to occupy his thoughts more and more. As though the years had not changed anything, his fantasies were of them both still young. He imagined that she had not rejected him and that she had married him after he had proposed. He dreamed of their being together and of his making love with her. Finally, he became so obsessed with Stella that he hired a private detective agency to find her.

A week ago, he had called her and, after a short conversation, had arranged a flight to Chicago where she now lived. He had arrived the day before and was now going to see her.

The bus came to a jarring halt, interrupting his thoughts once again. An elderly woman came slowly up the steps with a shopping bag just as the blond girl squeezed quickly by her and disappeared down the steps.

Edward looked out, momentarily blinded by the sun's glare, and he heard the roar of the bus as it took off again.

Once more he experienced the delight he had felt hearing Stella's voice over the phone. She had protested at first. She had not wanted him to see her grown old, but he had insisted.

As he saw the name of the street she lived on, he reached up and pulled the cord, alerting the bus driver that he wanted to get off. Edward stood up and braced himself for the stop.

It was warm but he put on his jacket anyway and pulled at his tie as he turned into the walk of an apartment building with paint peeling off the siding; its shabbiness startled him. He looked for her name above the tarnished brass mailboxes, then down at the gold watch Jean had given him. It was 3:30, the time he was to arrive. Edward rang the bell and waited.

He heard the buzzer and pushed the door open into the cool, dimly lit entry. He walked down the corridor until he found her apartment. He stood for a moment and raised his hand to knock when the door opened. His chest tightened.

How changed she was! Her beautiful face, now finely lined, her blonde hair now gray, wrapped around her head into a bun. Her blue eyes paled, her slim body thickened. She wore a flowered long-sleeved blouse tucked into a long black skirt.

"Come in, Edward. It's so good to see you." Her voice trembled slightly.

"Stella," he greeted her, as he looked into her face, and took hold of both her hands. He had prepared a little speech but now could not remember what he had wanted to say.

He followed her into a cool, dim little parlor.

"Edward, please sit down," she said, leading him to a red velvet sofa. He looked around the room filled with elaborate Victorian furniture too large for the small space.

"I have just made some tea," Stella said.

Her head bent as she occupied herself with the teapot, ice, and glasses. A wisp of hair free from her bun fell across her face. He watched her hands while she poured the tea into the ice-filled glasses. She handed him his tea then sat down across from him, smiling, her face suddenly appearing young to him.

"We are very old acquaintances, Edward."

"Yes, Stella, very old acquaintances indeed."

He nodded, his mind going back again to another warm summer afternoon long ago; in his tennis whites he came, two-steps at a time, up the wide wooden stairs of the hotel and across the spacious verandah lined with green canvas lounge chairs. He pulled open the wide screen door and stepped into the vast, redwood-paneled lobby. Inside, it was cool and dim. Fragrant dinner smells filled the air.

"Edward," Stella said, bringing him back, "do you recall our afternoon teas, so long ago?"

"Yes," he replied, remembering the first day she called to him from across the lobby.

"Hel-loo, Edward, come have some tea with me."

At first, he had only been able to see her outline, blond hair, pale blue dress. He'd gone to her.

"My goodness, you look hot. Here," she said, handing him her handkerchief, "you are all sweaty."

He wiped his face and picked up his glass, taking a long drink. Then he held her handkerchief to his nose, inhaling her perfume.

"Edward..." Stella said, bringing him back from his reverie.

"I was remembering, Stella, when we had tea together that summer."

She looked down at her lap and then out the window through ecru lace curtains. She blew her nose and held her handkerchief there a moment. He watched as she took a deep breath, then looked up at the ceiling. He could tell from her expression that she was trying not to cry.

"Have you had a happy life, Edward?"

"Yes," he replied, "I have had a good life."

And then he told her about his wife, Jean, and of her recent death. And of his three boys, all attorneys and now partners in the firm he had founded. He told her of his daughters-in-law and his nine grandchildren. He talked about the big house he had built and of his great enjoyment in gardening. He didn't mention that his pleasure in gardening was an enjoyment that seemed to elude him now.

Stella asked many questions about the details of his life.

"Do you have a photo of Jean and your boys?"

"Who do the boys look like?"

"How old are your grandchildren?"

"What are their names?"

"Do you see them often?"

"Have your sons turned out the way you wanted?"

Edward paused and was quiet for a moment thinking of how comfortable he felt, a contentment he had rarely experienced in the past. He was not distracted by his law practice, his family, his house, by anything, and answered her easily and with pleasure.

"It is so lovely to be here talking with you, Stella," he said.

"Edward, did you love Jean?" she asked suddenly.

It caught him off guard. What an unexpected question. He started to say yes, then stopped. Why had she asked that?

He had lived with his wife for forty-two years. He had grieved when she died, but he had known for a long time that he didn't love her, not as he had loved Stella.

"No," he said, "we had a pleasant relationship, but I didn't love Jean."

It surprised him, hearing himself say those words, but he felt bold and continued.

"When I was young, I fell deeply in love with you and when it didn't work out, I vowed never to let it happen again."

"How do you mean, Edward?"

He looked away from her and was quiet for a moment.

"I closed off a part of me. I didn't want to be hurt that way ever again. Too painful. Much too painful."

She nodded. They were both quiet for several moments.

"I did very well and advanced quickly in the law firm. The nearer to thirty I became the stronger I felt the urge to start a family. It seemed so natural for me to marry one of the senior partner's daughters at my firm, the absolute right thing to do career-wise..." His voice trailed off. He looked down at his hands, quiet for a moment.

"Please, go on," she said.

"Well," he continued, "her parents and my parents were both eager for the match. So, marrying her was the easiest thing to do. I didn't really want the marriage, but I let the wedding happen anyway."

Funny, he thought, how often these days he had a hard time

remembering something that happened the day before but could quickly and easily recall events and feelings of fifty years ago.

"From the beginning, I wasn't happy. Oh, that's not entirely true. I loved the boys. Jean was a good mother, she kept a nice house for me. We had friends, standing in the community. But our relationship never felt right. I was always waiting for something to happen. I don't even know if she felt the same way, we never discussed it."

He paused, "This is the first time I've ever talked about it with anyone."

Stella nodded.

"We weren't really intimate. We had sex and Jean gave birth to three beautiful boys, but after the children were born, Jean lost interest. She was nice, she obliged me," he paused looking down at his long fingers resting on his knees. "I had an affair for many years with a secretary in our office. She was a great comfort to me. I don't think Jean ever knew."

"What happened, Edward? Why didn't you leave her?"

"I don't know. We had a very busy life, active all the time with the boys, building the firm, friends, charities, community activities, then the grandchildren. It seemed there was never enough time or the right time. Then Jean became ill, and after two difficult years, she passed away. My longtime relationship also ended when my wife died."

He smiled and thought how sad, how tragic life can be. He smoothed his hair.

"I always dreamed about this, about being able to talk together like we are now."

The words flowed from him, giving him a sense of relief; he was finally expressing feelings that were truths for him that he had denied. He thought that perhaps the reason he had always felt such a pervading sense of regret was because he had never done anything about his relationship with Jean.

As he talked on, a sudden calm washed over him, one he'd rarely felt before.

It was quiet in the room except for the loud even ticking of the clock on the fireplace mantel. He sipped the iced aromatic tea and enjoyed his new tranquility.

He looked at Stella and saw that she was weeping, her narrow shoulders hunched and shaking.

"Oh, please forgive me, I don't know what it is I'm crying about. I think seeing you after so many years has made me feel very emotional and sad. I've felt this way ever since you called."

She wiped her eyes with a delicate lace handkerchief. She drew a long trembling breath. "I want you to know a little about my life too, Edward." She hesitated a moment. "I married well, to Graham Evans."

He had long ago known whom she had married. Graham had been socially elite, rich, the governor's son.

"The first several years, I was very happy. We traveled, we built a lovely house, we had lots of friends and parties. We had five children: four girls and a boy."

She stared out the window and her voice lowered.

"Then came the stock market crash and, well, it was as though none of us could handle the shock of losing everything. Father killed himself and Graham began drinking heavily. After five terrible years of his out-of-control drunkenness, he died, leaving me nearly destitute with still young children."

"Stella, I had no idea. I'm so sorry," Edward murmured. He was filled with sadness for her. He now understood the great change in Stella.

"I sold what I could, and then I went to work, in an accounting office, taking dictation, managing things. I supported everyone, including Mother."

She was quiet a moment, her head nodding a little as if affirming her memories. "The war came and I lost my only son." Her voice broke and she paused, but then went on. "The girls all went to college, had careers, got married. I did my duty as a mother. I too have grandchildren who bring me great joy. Really," she paused, "my greatest happiness."

The silence was heavy, the ticking of the clock steady and loud. Her hands clasped the lace handkerchief in her lap. "I'm very moved by the feelings you expressed for me, Edward," she looked away from him. "I'm most grateful."

For some time, he had been watching her rounded yet still graceful body, her delicate hands. She was still lovely to him. Slowly, feeling the pain in his joints, he got up and crossed over to her. She looked up at him as he sat down next to her. "Give me your hand, Stella."

She gave her hand to him, and he, holding it in both of his, brought it to his lips, pressing it there, feeling her trembling slightly. Then he gently took her into his arms.

After a time, he leaned away from her, took her face in his hands, and kissed her very gently on the lips. He arose and walked toward the door; she accompanied him. They stood awkwardly at the open doorway.

"Edward, are you disappointed in me? I mean, do you still feel about me as you did so many years ago?"

He took her hands again and placed them for a few moments against his lips. He touched her soft gray hair and looked down at her. "Yes," he smiled, "I do, I truly do!" He put his arms around her and they held each other close.

Then he remembered that he'd read about the Picasso exhibit at the museum.

"Would you like to go with me to the museum tomorrow?" he asked. The question hung in the air for only a moment.

"Yes, Edward," she said, "I would love to."

He turned and walked down the hallway, out the door, and into the street. The sudden brightness of the afternoon startled him and he took a deep breath.

Walking faster, he hardly noticed the pain in his joints as he whistled a song he and Stella had danced to fifty years ago, remembering the words as though it were yesterday.

I'm in the mood for love...Simply because you're near me...Funny but when you're near me...I'm in the mood for love...

THE AWARD

Sara opened her eyes and stretched both arms over her head. She had slept well. Very well. She lay relaxed, eyes gently closed, enjoying her sense of well-being. How fortunate she felt. It was almost scary; could she be too lucky? Nothing truly bad had ever happened to her.

Today was the day she was receiving the Summit Award from her company, Strata Environmental, for her outstanding work on saving the habitat for the endangered New England cottontail rabbit. Nominated by her colleagues and selected by a committee of her peers, she epitomized the company's values of integrity, respect, and high performance.

She brought her knees up to her chest (like her personal trainer had taught her) and rolled gracefully out of bed, stood up, and looked at the view from her bedroom window.

Beautiful! Blue sky, blue water, gray mountains, seagulls diving for fish — how great her jog was going to be, she thought. She looked forward to work. The whole day was going to be perfect.

She dressed, put on her socks and slippers, and walked into the kitchen. She opened the food cabinet and checked her supply of healthy energy drinks, selecting a Hiko coconut water with mango. She checked its contents on the label: potassium, magnesium, calcium, phosphorous — nothing healthier than that, she thought. Sara sat down to put on her new running shoes, drank her Hiko, took her jacket off the coat tree and slipped it on, checking to see that her credit card was still in the pocket as she went out the door.

Sara jogged gently, preserving her knees, across the street, down one block, then into the park and onto the jogging path. She felt content and strong. She had always honored her body and put her health first. Her Grandfather Abe, whom she loved very much, used to say, "Sara, the most important thing in your life is your health, always preserve it. Without that you can't accomplish much."

And so she did. She ate "right," no animal meat, lots of fruits and vegetables, always got seven to eight hours of sleep every night. She had a personal strength trainer, jogged every day, and did yoga three times a week. She felt good about herself, knowing her healthy lifestyle had paid off.

She came out of the park and waited at the stoplight, thinking about the chai tea latte she was going to have in just three blocks. She crossed the street and jogged by shop windows where she looked at her reflection as she passed. She liked the way she looked: long legs, slim waist, blond hair pulled into a ponytail bouncing up and down under her stylish cap.

Suddenly, she bumped into a woman in front of her.

"Sorry," she said but was really bothered by how disgusting, out of shape, and grossly fat — at least three-hundred pounds — the woman was. As Sara jogged by her, she also noticed the woman's ugly shoes and enormous, loose flowered shirt, and she decided to turn around and jog back a few steps in order to see the woman face forward. She was confronted by flabby jowls, straight brown hair, and huge flopping breasts. To top it off, the fat lady was sipping on a straw from a giant sweet soda drink. Sara turned back around and picked up her pace as she jogged toward the corner. She couldn't stop thinking about the offensive giant soft drink the woman had in her hand.

Sara was at the corner when she turned around and, jogging in place, she impulsively yelled at the fat lady, "Stop drinking that junk — that's why you're so fat!"

Sara then stepped backward off the curb into the street, so she didn't see the truck making a right turn as it slammed right into her: *crash!*

The fat lady, lumbering toward the corner, joined the shocked crowd and stared.

THE AFFAIR

"I brought you some wine, Cynthia darling, your favorite Chardonnay," Jerold said. As he handed his wife the glass, he saw she was chatting with her friend Janet.

"Janet, can I get you a glass?" he asked.

"Yes, I'd like that," Janet answered. "You're so considerate."

"Cynthia, you have the nicest husband!" Janet whispered, smiling and nodding at another guest.

"Yes," Cynthia replied, thinking again that maybe he was too perfect, too reliable, not exciting enough.

Jerold returned with Janet's wine. The two women, long-time close friends, hugged each other as they heard the dinner bell.

"Okay, everyone," said their hostess, "dinner is served."

Cynthia was happy to see the Episcopal minister, Reverend Robert Cortland, whom she had known for years, standing next to the chair where she was to be seated.

"Hello, Cynthia," he smiled at her. "You look beautiful tonight. What luck to have such a lovely dinner partner!"

She smiled and began to wonder what was happening as she looked at him. She could feel her heart beating. "That's such a nice thing to say to me, the best thing I've heard today actually!"

She studied his face as if for the first time, his fair skin and large blue eyes. He brushed a lock of his straight, graying blonde hair from his forehead and held her chair out as she sat down.

"So, what are you reading these days?" he asked her. They shared an interest in reading novels.

"I'm reading a new novel, *The Engagement*," Cynthia replied. "It's essentially about possession and obsession. Pretty enthralling."

"Tell me more about it," Robert said. "I'm looking for a compelling read."

As she started to explain the complex, psychological thriller, the first course arrived.

"Soup's delicious, don't you think?" he asked.

"Yes, my favorite, lobster bisque," she responded.

Throughout dinner, they talked about the writers they each loved, especially the Russians.

"And Robert, I know your favorite novel because it's my favorite, too. *Anna Karenina.*"

They looked at each other, smiling, and repeated in unison their favorite line from the opening of the book: *"Happy families are all alike; every unhappy family is unhappy in its own way."*

Cynthia looked down the long elegant table at the dancing lights from the candles and the attractive guests talking animatedly to one another, her husband among them. She listened to the soft hum of conversation. It was as though everything around her was background; she was only interested in Robert and was enjoying the new feelings of excitement she was experiencing.

"Are you getting used to being single?" Cynthia asked. They talked about his recent divorce.

"We were married for over fifteen years; it's been over a year and I'm only just beginning to get over it." He paused. "I'm also concerned about how the divorce is affecting my status in the church."

"Yes," Cynthia replied, "I know divorce is not politically correct for a minister of the church."

"The divorce coupled with my positive stand on gay ministers," he paused. "Well, I've been put on leave from St. Paul's Cathedral, and it's very possible that I may be assigned to a smaller church."

She could see the pain in his eyes and placed her hand on his for a moment as it rested on the table.

Cynthia felt the electricity from his touch and wondered again what was happening to her. And why now? She and Jerold had known Robert for ten years; she had seen him many times at fundraisers and in church, where he was their pastor. But now she was seeing him with very different eyes; she was enamored, and a little dizzy, perhaps from the wine?

As dessert was being served, her husband looked at her from across the table, eyebrows raised, and mimed the words, "Are you ready to go?"

Cynthia stared back at him and shook her head no; she didn't want to leave the party.

Jerold leaned toward her, "That's certainly not like you, Cynthia," he chuckled.

She smiled and shrugged her shoulders. Usually they were the first to leave from what Cynthia called endless dinner parties.

She looked at Robert in his clerical collar; the notion of being intimate, of making love with a person close to God, made her want to touch him. She adjusted her chair a little closer and felt her leg touch his. Robert looked at her, she smiled and didn't move away.

Jerold, Robert, and Cynthia were the last to leave. She didn't want to say goodbye to Robert and for the first time in years began to feel the unceasing heaviness within her begin to wane. Her therapist told her the anxiety she felt was because she was bored and needed to find new challenges.

 She stood a moment and looked at her friend's tastefully furnished entry — the pale green vase perfectly placed on the walnut console table, the elegant Persian rug and pale ivory walls. She took a deep breath and hugged her hostess.

"Thank you so much Lucy, what a lovely evening!"

In bed that night, with her husband beside her, she thought about Robert and how electrified her body had felt being near him. Like a teenager, she thought about having imaginary phone conversations with him.

She knew that boldly propositioning a man to have sex with her was outrageous, but she could not get it out of her mind. Two days later, Jerold told her he needed to go out of town on business for a week and that she should invite a friend to attend the symphony in his place; her feeling was that the affair was meant to be. As soon as she dropped the children at school, she called Robert.

"Hi, Robert," she said, pausing a moment, hoping he would recognize her voice. "This is Cynthia Howard, how are you?"

She was shaking and felt scared but told him she had an extra ticket for the symphony on Friday and asked if he would like to join her.

"I'd like that very much," Robert replied, and they made arrangements to meet in front of Symphony Hall.

She replaced the phone in its cradle, feeling her hand shake. All week she could think of nothing else but seeing him again.

On symphony night, when they met, Robert looked around. "Where's Jerold?" he asked.

"He's away," she replied. "You're sitting in his seat."

She felt strong, excited, and, at the same time, scared. Sitting next to him in the vast Davies Symphony Hall filled with people, she could feel the heat of her body as they touched elbows briefly now and then on the shared armrest. Listening to the refined and elegant sounds of a Mozart sonata, Cynthia felt a calm she never wanted to end.

She loved music and attended the symphony weekly during the season but had never felt music as deeply as this night. Before they parted that evening, she asked him if he would like to have lunch with her on Sunday at the conservatory in the park.

"It's my favorite place to be," she added.

The next day, backing out of the garage, Cynthia paused and ran through her list of tasks for the day.

The children were organized, and she had completed all her phone calls for their annual school carnival. Now she was driving to Union Square to have lunch with her friend Janet. She switched on a classical music station and was pleased to hear her favorite Chopin etude.

Cynthia slowed to stop at a red light. She reached up and tilted the rearview mirror to see that her make-up and hair were perfect. She watched an attractive young woman in the crosswalk pushing a baby carriage with one hand while holding the hand of a cute three- or four-year-old blond boy as they crossed in front of her.

That's me, she thought as she remembered the familiar heaviness she had felt since early on in her marriage, a heaviness that was now dissipating since the night she'd had dinner at Lucy's.

She had had loving parents and old-fashioned immigrant grandparents from Europe who had convinced her that achievement for a woman was being married to a successful man; rich is what they actually meant. A happy, successful woman was one who had a husband who could provide a lovely home, children, and expensive jewelry and furs.

She had fulfilled their aspirations for her. She had met her husband at a dinner party where she and her date were seated across from Jerold. They chatted and when he asked her where she worked, she gave him the office building address.

The next day, at work for her attorney brother-in-law, she was surprised when Jerold walked in the door.

"How did you know where I worked?" Cynthia exclaimed.

"You told me which building, so I checked every office until I found you here on the ninth floor — I'm glad it was not the 21st!" Jerold exclaimed with a wide smile.

And so that was the way it had begun. Jerold was twenty years her senior and a successful businessman, CEO of his grandfather's contracting business, tall, solidly built, hair beginning to gray at the temples. Dark piercing eyes, a very good dancer, well-known in the city and already thinking of a political career, as he was president of the Arts Commission. She was charmed, and within the year they had married.

Jerold was successful and rich. So, what was wrong, why was she so unhappy? Not only had she achieved all that she was raised to accomplish, she had no complaints like other women she knew, who thought their hips were too big or their breasts too small. She was pleased with her dark, naturally curly hair, slender figure, and perfect nose.

What was she doing in the therapist's office, four days a week, expressing her angst? Dr. Hershey called it "free-floating anxiety," and suggested she and Jerold attend some supplemental group sessions, which actually made her feel worse, because not only did she learn that Jerold had been unfaithful, engaging in several short love affairs since their marriage began, she was able to see and hear "real" issues people had to deal with.

She thought of the group session when she'd heard one woman's anguished confession about the incestuous relationship she was forced into with her father. Cynthia felt embarrassed to be there when she herself had no complaints that came close to those she heard from the others in the group.

And now, thinking about Robert, she couldn't fathom the sad feelings she remembered having once had. She thought how lucky she was to have accepted Lucy's invitation for dinner. What if she hadn't?

Cynthia was afraid she was late to meet Robert and jogged the short distance from her car to the conservatory in the park. She arrived out of breath and did not see him. She stopped and looked around and thought about what she wanted: to go to bed with Robert. She had not talked about it with her therapist because she knew what he would say — that she should think it over, not let her emotions cloud her judgment. She didn't want to hear it; she knew an affair was wrong and didn't care.

"Hello!" She turned to see Robert walking toward her, his arm swinging freely over his head as he waved at her. He was so tall and attractive! His long, pale straight hair made her think of the fairy-tale princes she read about to her children. She took a deep breath as he approached her.

"Hi, Robert," she said.

"Hello," he said again, bending and brushing her cheek lightly with a kiss.

She looked up at him for a moment. "Come with me," she said softly.

Cynthia led the way into the conservatory. She had always loved the distinctly Victorian architecture, the curved, painted white glass, the gravel paths.

Stepping inside, they were surrounded by the strong scent of earth and moist leaves. She inhaled deeply, enjoying the sensuousness of being there with him, hearing his feet crunching the gravel path behind her.

"Hey, slow down," Robert said.

"Sorry," she said, looking up at him. He took her hand and she shivered. They walked together through the conservatory and its bright, humid, perfumed atmosphere.

They walked quietly, holding hands, stopping frequently to gaze at the exotic plants. Standing side by side, they watched the lava plant with its shades of reds and greens and beautiful slim pointed leaves. The diffused light and warmth through the glass panels felt soft and luxurious. The exit was obscured because the path they were on was surrounded by tall Ficus plants with wild trumpet vines crawling unchecked over the branches. They stood quietly, eyes closed, their bodies absorbing the atmosphere, inhaling the dense, deeply perfumed air surrounding them.

When Cynthia opened her eyes, she saw the bright light at the end of the path and knew they were near the exit. They walked to her car to pick up the lunch she had packed. Cynthia led the way along a path into the park looking for a place to picnic. Here and there gardeners worked in pairs, clipping, weeding, and tending the gardens. Sprinklers whirred, spraying water onto the ground. Birds chirped in every tree, and small squirrels jumped from limb to limb. The sky was cloudless and very blue.

She closed her hands into fists and pressed her fingernails into her palms to remind herself that she was really there, looking at him, walking with him, listening to him talk. Cynthia felt scared and excited at the same time in anticipation of what might happen.

"There is a perfect spot to eat," he said, pointing to a grassy place on a knoll away from the path, under a large tree. He carried the picnic basket and she followed, watching the movement of his body as he walked. They spread a blanket and drank the wine and ate the bread, cheese, and first cherries of the season that she had brought.

"Cynthia, why did you call me?" he asked her without warning. She hesitated, feeling her face flush.

"This is the first time that I have done anything like this," she paused, her heart pounding, and looked away from his face. "I just wanted to be with you."

She felt his arms encircle her as he pulled her down on the blanket. "Cynthia, I have been attracted to you since the first time I saw you, years ago. You are so beautiful."

Now she looked full into his face; she could smell his skin and warm breath, his large eyes mesmerizing her. Then he was kissing her. She felt starved for him, her lips pressed hard against his, her body trembling.

"Please, Robert..." she dared.

"Yes," he said. "Anything."

"Make love to me." He pulled away, slightly, still holding her tightly.

"Here?"

She laughed and gently lay back on the soft grass. "No," she said, her breathing still ragged, "not here. I think I'm too cautious for that."

"I'm glad you didn't say yes," he whispered into her ear. "I don't have the nerve, either."

They lay there together, enveloped in the warmth of the sun, her head on his shoulder, her eyes closed. "Can I see you tomorrow?" she asked before they parted.

Cynthia finished her tasks and phone calls before she walked out the patio doors into the garden. The light rain had stopped. She listened to the collected giant raindrops dripping through the branches of the trees, plunking dully and rhythmically on the ground. She saw that the stepping stones set into the grass had turned into small round puddles of water. The hum of automobiles passing on the street outside the garden wall, tires squishing on the wet pavement, was the only intrusion into her thoughts.

Near the garden wall, hanging from an ancient cherry tree, was her children's swing. One of the ropes had broken, and the wooden seat hung tilted, its end touching the ground. It had been that way for weeks. Gazing at the broken rope, she knew she had not loved her husband for years. She looked down at her watch. It was a quarter to one, time to go.

Cynthia walked into the garage and unlocked the door of her pale green Jaguar, a recent gift from Jerold. She backed slowly out of the garage, knowing that what she was doing was not right, but feeling like a naughty child, unable to do anything but go to Robert.

Her heart beat with excitement as she climbed the stairs to his apartment. He opened the door and she stepped inside. She looked down the hallway into the neat living room. He was standing near her; she could smell his skin.

He put his arms around her and she clung to him; she felt intoxicated.

"Will you come to my bedroom with me?" he whispered. He led the way down the long hallway and she watched him walk as she had in the park.

They entered his bedroom. Sheer curtains danced to-and-fro from the breeze of the open window. He lay down on his large bed. She undressed near him, at his bedside. She felt no embarrassment as she stood naked, her clothes around her feet. He stretched his arms out to her and she fell on him, kissing him, feeling his tongue in her mouth, his lips pressed hard against hers. She pressed her body against him and felt overwhelmed by her desire and passion for him.

"Cynthia, I have thought of nothing but you since yesterday in the park."

"And I have thought only about you," she whispered. She undressed him, admiring his muscular, smooth body. They made love with a passion that was new to her. Her orgasm was long and very intense.

She looked at the clock next to the bed, and saw it was time to pick the children up at school. Swinging her legs over the side of the bed, she started to stand, but as she did, her knees folded and she fell back onto the bed, into his arms. She had never felt anything like this total sensuality and knew she could not go on with her life as it had been.

Their lovemaking was passionate in a way that Cynthia had never experienced before. Robert became the focus of her life and she rearranged everything to be with him. They saw one another every day, and they made love every day.

They were together in the afternoons before she picked the children up from school. They made love to music; their favorite was the sensuous "Carmina Burana." Being with Robert became an addiction. They made love every day. Coming home after being with Robert was exciting. She even managed weekends away with him. She was leading a double life — one that was like a sexy novel yet appeared extremely conventional.

Since the group therapy sessions where she'd learned her husband was having brief affairs with women, it no longer bothered her, though she did feel guilty about the time she spent with Robert and away from her children. She rationalized her behavior by thinking that because she was happier now, her children would benefit from having a happier mother.

It was not long before she took her closest friends into her confidence; they covered for her with phone or text messages or written invitations to join them for spa weekends or nights out with the girls, which she showed to her husband. She became adept at covering her absences from Jerold and the children.

In the beginning, the affair helped Cynthia tolerate her life. There was an excitement to the double life she was living. The impatience and boredom she felt in the past at dinner parties with her husband and on Sundays with her in-laws was now tolerable; she felt the excitement she remembered as a child when she did something mean to her sister without being caught.

Lying in bed next to Robert one afternoon after their passionate lovemaking, Cynthia said, "Robert, I'm so in love with you, you are always on my mind, just like the song." She felt Robert's lips on the back of her neck and shivered.

People began to talk. *The City Tribune*'s gossip columnist, Harry Cantor, mentioned them one weekday morning:

"The Palomar Writer's Conference last weekend was made more interesting with the presence of the wife of a prominent businessman and a quite liberal well-known clergyman..."

Cynthia didn't allow herself to consider the consequences; she didn't care. It was exciting, she was doing something bad, and she enjoyed every moment of it. Robert sent her intimate, sexually explicit love letters, which she would read over and over again, relishing the passion he expressed and treasuring the way he felt about her.

She placed the letters in a large, unmarked manila envelope, which she put in the back of the lower drawer of her desk.

She still visited her therapist, but now only once a week. While there, she talked about Robert, their love affair, her double life, her lack of guilt and anxieties about whether it would all endure. The absence of intimacy she had felt with Jerold no longer troubled her. Robert filled all her needs.

Now, when she dropped the children at school, she no longer felt the anxiety she had felt before, the sense of *what now?* Shopping or maybe lunch with...? Her interest in organizing charity events had diminished. She simply thought of her next meeting with Robert and her happiness was restored.

Her daughter Regina was not doing well in school. Her report card reflected a lack of attention in class as well as poor grades. One morning, the school called to report that Regina had gotten into a fight with a classmate and was being suspended for three days. Cynthia picked her up from school and brought her home.

"Regina, what's going on? Why did you get into a fight with Nancy? She's been your best friend forever."

"She's not my best friend anymore and I hate her! She said her mother told her that you were never home and that she couldn't have a sleepover at my house anymore." Regina started to cry and when Cynthia tried to put her arms around her she screamed, "Don't touch me. I hate you, too!" and she ran into her room, slamming the door.

After that, Cynthia decided to begin psychotherapy sessions for Regina and made an appointment with a well-respected child therapist. When she told Regina that the therapist would be someone she could talk to and maybe help figure out why she was not happy, Regina screamed, "I am not crazy! I don't want to talk to anybody!"

Cynthia was firm and often pulled Regina by the hand into the therapist's office.

One Saturday when Cynthia was away for yet another weekend charity "conference," Regina attempted to talk with her father. "Daddy, why isn't Mommy ever home? She's always away."

"Look, sweetheart," Jerold said, giving her a hug, "your mom is very busy with her charity work and her friends. You will understand better when you are a grown-up."

The following Saturday, after Cynthia left for the weekend, Regina, feeling lonely, started going through her mother's desk drawers. Her father was out, and only the two *au pairs* were at home looking after her and her brother. After going through her mother's drawers in the bedroom, she went into the home office and began looking through the desk drawers there, where she found a large manila envelope. She opened the envelope and saw it was filled with dozens of smaller envelopes.

She opened the first envelope and began to read. It was a letter from Robert. Was that the Robert who was the minister of their church whom she had known since she was a little girl? The Robert who came to their house for dinner, and who everyone was talking about when he got divorced from his wife? She had heard her parents talking about how he had nearly lost his job in the church.

Regina read one letter after another. She didn't understand all that he had written, since the only things she knew about sex she'd read in her mother's library, novels about grown-ups. Regina was confused and began to cry as she thought of what to do about her discovery. After a while she blew her nose and looked at the letters scattered on the floor and decided to give them to her dad when he came home that night.

When Cynthia returned late Sunday night, Jerold was sitting at the kitchen table. She looked at his face and knew something was wrong.

"Hi, Jerold," she hesitated. "Sorry I'm so late. There was a big accident on the freeway and..."

Cynthia could feel the sweat break out under her arms; her knees felt weak. Jerold looked at her with an anger she had not seen before.

"You're a fucking cheat, Cynthia. I understand why you'd do this to me, Christ, you know I've never been faithful, but the kids...that's what I'm having a hard time understanding." He stared at her as she sat down across from him.

"Why did you save his goddamned letters?" he yelled, and got up from his chair, shouting at her now. "Regina gave them to me last night when I came home from the golf tournament!"

"Oh my God!" Cynthia began to cry. She bent over the table, cradling her head in her arms and sobbed. Standing over her, Jerold shouted, "I'm moving out tonight. I can't stand to be anywhere near you!"

Cynthia was crying. "Maybe I wanted the marriage to be over, Jerold. It's all I talked about in therapy. I've never been happy. I'm sorry."

He was standing next to her. Cynthia could feel his body heat and rage. "You'd better hurry up and find another sucker to support you in the style you're accustomed to because I'll be god-dammed if you're getting anything beyond child support." He paused and then continued, "I'm asking you again, why would you do something so stupid as to keep those letters from that asshole priest?"

Cynthia kept her head down and cried; she had nothing to say.

"I'll send the warehouse guys here tomorrow to pack up my stuff."

She heard him walk out of the room and the front door slam. The marriage was over and even though she had come to the realization that it was what she wanted, Cynthia felt frightened.

Still seated in the kitchen, she cried, and thought about what to do. Call her therapist? No, call Robert. No, she really did not want to talk to Robert. Finally, she called her friend Janet — she could tell her anything.

Janet answered, "Cynthia, it's almost midnight, are you okay?"

"No, Janet, not really...I need to talk to you. Regina gave Robert's letters to Jerold this weekend while I was away, and Jerold just left, he wants a divorce!"

"Oh, my God, Cynthia, what are you going to do?"

The next day, Cynthia sat in the car outside the children's school waiting to pick them up. She thought how really proud she was of her daughter, who, not even twelve years old yet, had submitted her original dollhouse design to the seventh-grade junior design contest and won first prize. And how, even without coaching, she'd gotten all A's in her schoolwork. She saw Regina come out of the middle school gates and walk down to the kindergarten to wait for Steven.

Soon Steven came running out, backpack hanging off his shoulder, one knee sock down around his ankle. Cynthia watched as he grabbed the outstretched hand of his sister while they both ran toward her.

"Mommy, I have some really good news," Regina said as she climbed into the car. "I have been picked to run for class president and I don't think anyone is going to run against me!"

"That's because they don't know how stinky you are," Steven said, "and how you wouldn't play with me when I got my new...."

"Okay, okay, kids please don't fight, let's get an ice cream and go to the park. I have something to tell you," Cynthia said as they got into the car.

Seated on the bench in the park with Regina and Steven on either side of her, Cynthia felt her eyes fill with tears. "I want you to know that Daddy and I both love you very much."

Regina started to cry. "Uh oh, you're going to tell us something bad and I think it is something I did..."

"No darling, it is nothing you have done, it is just that Daddy and I are going to live in separate houses..." She began to cry as the children moved closer to her.

She hugged them. "Things are not going to be that different...you will still see both of us a lot. Daddy is moving into Grandma's building so he will be close by and I have decided not to do so much charity work, so I'll be at home more."

"Why?" asked Steven, "I want Daddy to live with us..."

"Yeah, I want him to live with us too," said Regina.

And the questions went on until there were no more, and she and the children sat quietly, their heads on their mother's shoulder.

Arriving home, Cynthia thought that everything was going to be okay as she watched the children jump out of the car and run up to the front door. *I'm not even missing Robert*, she thought, a little amazed at how and why everything seemed to be working out.

That evening, when Cynthia arrived at the Farley Café, she

was asked if she had a reservation. "No, I believe my friend is already here."

She looked across the room and saw Janet in a booth; she walked over and sat down.

"So," Janet said, "what happened?"

"Well, you know last night I told you about Regina giving Robert's letters to Jerold..."

Janet nodded, "Yes, too horrible to think about."

"Terrible scene with Jerold," Cynthia said.

Janet's eyes filled with tears, "I'm so sorry."

The waiter appeared. Annoyed at the interruption, Janet said, "We'll both have the chicken salad."

"My parents came over this afternoon," Cynthia paused, "and they told me they would help me if I needed to supplement my income. Actually, my mother said until you find another husband."

Janet raised her eyebrows.

"Yes, she really said that."

"So, Cynthia, what are you going to do?"

"This is the first time in my life that I am really free. I want to go to work, to finally, for the first time, take care of myself."

"Cynthia, why go to work if you don't have to? You know I've always worked because I've had to, but I would love to be a lady of leisure if I could..."

"Janet, no, I need something more, a challenge, I want to accomplish something. Remember how much I loved furnishing my house? I'm thinking I might go back to school, study design, become a decorator."

"That sounds exciting. Big changes though." Janet smiled.

"I think I'm ready," Cynthia said as their salads arrived. "My next big challenge is to tell Robert it's over. I've talked about it with Dr. Hershey. We both think that my intoxication with Robert was a way of getting out of my marriage. In other words, I didn't have the courage to tell Jerold that I wasn't happy and wanted the marriage to end."

The next morning, as Cynthia was planning what she was going to say to Robert, he called. "Cynthia, I have something to tell..."

She interrupted him, "Robert, I have to tell you something..."

"Cynthia," he interrupted her, "please, let me finish. I have just been offered a parish in upstate New York where my kids live, and I've decided to take it. I would love you to come," he hesitated, "but I know how you feel about being a reverend's wife."

"I think it is time, Robert," Cynthia responded quietly. "We've loved one another, and now maybe it is time for us to part. I feel sad, Robert, but happy that finally we are both moving on."

After she hung up the phone, Cynthia cried: for Robert, for Jerold, for her kids, and finally, for herself. "Why is life so fucking hard!" she said out loud to no one.

As the weeks passed, Cynthia became aware of new feelings, very different from how she'd felt her entire adult life. She wanted to be on her own, to take care of herself and her children, to be independent. She enrolled in design school and felt excited every day going to her classes.

She decided to sell her fur coats and gathered them into her arms. She knew they were valuable and she needed the income, but they were also symbolic of her old life. As she left the fur resale shop, she thought what a great feeling it was to get rid of those expensive coats.

Next came the wine cellar. Little by little she was leaving her old way of life behind. She called some friends she knew who could afford to buy the large cellar and she felt good about their enthusiasm for the wine. On the day she watched the truck leave with the wine, Cynthia felt energetic and full of expectation. She was in charge of her own life and loved the feeling.

Curiously, she had no need to see Dr. Hershey. She didn't even want to see him for a last time, and called to cancel her regular appointment.

She hung up the phone with no regrets.

One morning, after dropping the kids at school, she drove to the conservatory in the park. As she got out of her car and walked up the path, she thought of her first meeting there with Robert.

As she entered the building and once again fell under its spell, she began to relax and inhale the earth and plant fragrances. She stood for a while next to the orchids and studied their small faces. Each had a beautiful broad tongue with a delicate fork at the tip and wide-set eyes. Cynthia thought how perfect nature is, and then walked on along the path.

A MORNING PRAYER

Good morning, Sweet Jesus. First, I want to ask you to keep all my brothers and sisters in the world safe and free from hunger and sorrow.

I want to confess that I am not from Mérida where I live now in the Izamal Mexican Monastery, and that I have not suffered from hunger and misery like the people here have.

I grew up in the city of Los Angeles in the United States. I lived in a big house with my mother and father and sister and brother. We had a private swimming pool and a garage that fit all four of our expensive cars.

We had a driver, Jacques, whose wife, Madeleine, was our cook. They lived in the apartment over the garage. Keisha, a black lady, came once a week to polish our silver and do the ironing, and Harry Hoshino, our Japanese cleaning man, came three times a week to vacuum and clean our house. The two French au pair girls, Bibi and Clarice, took care of us and lived in the maids' rooms downstairs.

I was driven to school each day by Jacques, as were many of the other kids who went to Page, my expensive private school, where all the other kids were privileged and spoiled and expected and accepted everything they had.

We ate steak and lobster. We went to concerts and movies and parties. We bought new clothes each year for school and never thought about how much they cost. We went to Hawaii for Christmas and New Year's, and in January and February we went skiing in Verbier, Switzerland, where we had our own ski chalet.

And then one Christmas, we came here to Mérida, and my life changed.

I saw poor people, people who were hungry and wore raggedy clothes, with shoes that had tire treads instead of leather soles. Some were sitting by the road, arms outstretched, hands opened and reaching out begging for coins.

And for me, even worse, because I love all animals, were the packs of dogs, ribs showing through their fur, running through the village streets, with barefooted children throwing rocks after them.

I think I knew then I could never again be happy living the life I was born into, knowing there was such misery in the world.

When I told my parents what I wanted to do, they were very upset and told me that if I made a decision to live my life as a monk they would disinherit me, that I would not receive a share of their fortune as my sister and brother would. I told them that was okay, I could no longer be happy with so much when there were people in the world with so little.

And so, here I am, a simple monk serving God and the poor. Thank you, Sweet Jesus, for helping me find meaning in my life.

PLASTIC JESUS, PART 2

We are towed into a huge lot with a very high fence around it. I see crushed cars heaped one on top of another, a mountain of flattened, rusted metal.

As I watch from my place on the dashboard, a tall red crane picks up a flattened car just a few feet away, lifts it high in the air where it swings back and forth, then drops with a loud crash on top of the pile. Violet was right: I was seeing the world. I wonder what my replicas back on the glass shelf would think.

It's nice here, warm and sunny, and the scene outside is both scary and exciting to watch. There are so many cars. I wonder if it hurts to be crushed. Suddenly, I feel Violet's car begin to move and vibrate.

"Hey Joe, hold it!" shouts a deep voice. "I been wantin' one of them little statues for my truck; wait a minute."

The vibrating stops, I hear the door open, and feel a rough hand grab me. I only catch a brief glimpse of the man's huge paunch before he drops me into the pocket of his work jacket. He has a gray stubbly beard and a big red nose. I hear him pulling my stand off the dashboard. He drops it next to me. The pocket is loose and open and I am on my back, so I look up and see the sky and tree tops.

After a while, my new owner gets into his truck, puts my stand on the dashboard, and places me on the stand. I feel a little wobbly since my stand is not stuck on very tightly.

Sometime later, we pull into the parking lot of Pete's Bar & Grill. Still in the truck, my new owner takes a small red phone out of his pocket.

He dials a number and I can hear it ring two or three times before a child's voice says, "Hello?"

The guy turns me around so I can see his face. "Hi, sweetie pie," he says into the phone. "This is Daddy Henry. How is my baby tonight?" A child's voice replies, "I'm fine," and then says,

"Mommy and Daddy Joe and me were just having dinner."

Daddy Henry stares at me with a sad look that has me vibrating again.

"Okay, sweetie, I just wanted to say hello and hear your voice and tell you that I love you very much!"

Not waiting for a response, Daddy Henry clicks the phone off and sits for a while. Then I hear a big sigh as he gets out of his truck.

It's hours before Daddy Henry returns. He looks at me for a long time without saying anything. Then he closes his eyes and I see a tear run down his cheek. I try to imagine how I can help him. He finds his phone and dials a number, and the phone rings and rings. The phone falls onto the floor as he starts the engine.

As we drive into the dark night, I fall over and roll back and forth across the dashboard, making a knocking sound each time I hit the windshield. Instead of driving straight, we're weaving from one side of the road to the other. This goes on for a while when all of a sudden I see bright white headlights coming toward us and then our ride ends with a thunderous crash. I'm thrown down onto the passenger seat next to Daddy Henry who is spread out across it. I stare at his red face. His eyebrows are bushy and gray, his eyes flutter open and closed.

"Oh, Jesus, help me, help me," he cries over and over. "Don't let me die, I don't want to die, I don't want to die, help me, help me, Sweet Jesus!"

I feel it again, that deep tingling. How can I help? I so want to, but I can't make myself do anything. After a while he is quiet, and all I can hear is the sound of raindrops thumping on the roof.

Soon it is light and I see two policemen walking around the truck. They remove Daddy Henry's body and carefully replace me upright on the dashboard. "There ya go, Jesus," one of them says.

After a while, a large tow truck backs up in front of me, and I almost fall off my stand as the front of Daddy Henry's truck is lifted. We're towed to a garage.

A big, high-ceilinged room with cars surrounds me. Some cars are perched in the air on thick round poles, while others are on the floor next to me with workmen's legs sticking out from under the fronts and backs of the cars. The windows of my truck are open and there is a strong smell all around me. The men with sprayers call it paint. I like the way it smells.

I get used to the jiggling and jolting while they are working on my truck until one day it becomes very quiet and I realize that the repairs must be finished. Soon, one of the workers gets in, and drives us into a large parking lot where there are many other cars and trucks all parked in neat rows.

There is a sign high in the air that says "Marvelous Marvin's Used Cars." There are many small, colorful, triangular-shaped flags surrounding the sign and flying in the breeze. It is quiet and peaceful here with the sun shining through the windshield – more of the world that Violet promised I'd see.

END PART 2

THE NEW NEIGHBORS

Part 1

Agnes held onto the railing as she slowly climbed the stairs behind her sister. It was her first visit to a witch and she was nervous, dubious, and not very hopeful, even though Louise had said such wonderful things about Wyndsong. Louise waited at the top of the stairs to give Agnes a reassuring hug.

"Agnes, I promise, you're really going to enjoy this. Wyndsong is terrific, you'll see! And," Louise insisted, "she's going to solve all your problems."

It had all started a few months earlier, when Tom and Agnes Parker, who had lived on Deer Island for thirty-two years, were talking, as usual, about all the new people moving onto the island, buying houses, tearing them down, and building new mini-mansions in their place. In the mail that day was a letter from the Deer Island Planning Commission notifying the residents on Britton Avenue that the Harringtons, the Parkers' new next-door neighbors, were planning to build a pool house, and that in three weeks there would be a Planning Commission meeting where anyone could protest if they had any reason not to approve the project. Agnes showed the letter to Tom.

"That is strange," Tom said, "since they already have a pool house, which is only four or five years old. Remember the nice party we went to after our former neighbors, the Smiths, finished building it?"

"I most certainly do," said Agnes. "But now, the Harringtons want to tear it down and build a brand new two-thousand-square-foot pool house. And the worst part is that they don't want to build it in the old location, but they want it exactly where it totally obstructs our beautiful view! So instead of seeing the seagulls and the water, we'll be looking at another house."

"Well, we'll just have to protest; we'll go to that meeting and dispute it," Tom said, giving Agnes a reassuring kiss.

On the day of the meeting, as Agnes was leaving the house for her daily walk, she ran into Vivica Harrington.

"Hi, Agnes," Vivica said, walking purposefully toward her. "Are you coming to the meeting tonight? We haven't heard anything from you, so we've assumed you're okay with our project."

"Actually Vivica, we're not," Agnes replied, trying to sound pleasant. "Did you know that your new pool house will be blocking our view?"

"No, I didn't know that." Vivica sounded truly surprised. "We've been working with our architect and landscape team and because we haven't heard anything to the contrary, we just assumed everything was okay. In fact, we've been assured that we'll be approved. Also, I don't know if George has told you this or not, but we are planning to clean up and prune those scraggly old trees of yours on the property line, all at our expense." Vivica waited for the enormity of the gesture to sink in. "We thought that would be a nice neighborly thing for us to do. We'd wanted it to be a surprise, but..."

"Oh, Vivica, thank you so..." Agnes said.

"Whoa," Vivica interrupted, looking at her watch, "I need to get going, I can't be late for work. See you tonight."

Agnes remained where she was standing, mouth open, and watched as Vivica jumped into her white BMW SUV and roared away. Agnes felt insulted, but as she began to walk, she became aware of a new feeling: anger.

Later that morning, Tom started feeling chest pains, so they arranged to meet Dr. Boynton, their doctor of over thirty years, at the local hospital. They told him about the Planning Commission meeting that night, and why Tom was so stressed. The doctor gave Tom a prescription for Valium to help him relax.

"Call me tomorrow and let me know how you feel," he told Tom as the Parkers left.

With Tom having taken Valium during the day as per the

doctor's orders, when it was time for the Planning Commission meeting, Agnes asked him if he felt up to going. He assured her that he was fine and still feeling the anger from the morning's encounter with Vivica, Agnes didn't argue.

As the Parkers entered the meeting room in City Hall, they were confronted by a slideshow playing on a large movie screen, first depicting architectural plans, then changing to views of a finished house, then to the interior rooms, and back again to the plans, all accompanied by soft background music.

There were seven Planning Commission members, though three had to recuse themselves as they were the architect, contractor, and landscape designer for the Harringtons' pool-house project. Agnes held Tom's hand as a loud rap of the gavel brought the meeting to order.

Tom and Agnes watched as five people walked to the podium and introduced themselves as the team working on the proposed project from the architect's office. They were all young and attractive, their presentations energetic and impressive. After answering some questions from the Commission, they sat down and Vivica and George Harrington walked to the podium.

Agnes couldn't help admiring the tall, blonde, even-featured, smiling, and confident couple. They held hands and each spoke about how much it meant to them to be a part of the beautiful Deer Island community, how family was first, and how important it was to them to have a place where they could entertain out-of-doors with out-of-town family guests able to stay in the new, proposed pool house.

They ended their presentation with their offer to prune the neglected trees on their elderly neighbor's property at their expense. They were asked some questions about the project by the four un-recused members of the commission, and then sat down.

The Commission chairman asked if the Parkers would like to speak. Tom Parker took a long time getting up out of his seat and walking to the microphone, which he had trouble adjusting, so someone in the front row assisted him.

"Members of the Planning Commission, ladies and gentlemen," he began, "we are here tonight to respectfully protest the plans for this pool-house project and ask that the Harringtons reconsider a plan that is less majestic and that doesn't block our view. You may not know that essentially our view is worth more than our house, and by taking away that view, our property value is greatly diminished." He paused. "Why not place the new pool house where the old pool house was, so it will not affect or diminish our property value?"

His short talk, in comparison to the Harringtons' carefully crafted presentation, seemed halting and incomplete, and he sometimes missed speaking into the microphone completely.

George Harrington, with his slight beard and fashionably shaved head, stood up and walked back to the mic, gently shouldering Tom to the side.

"May I address your concerns?" He proceeded to talk again about how important family was and that if they placed the new pool house where the original pool house was, as their neighbor Tom suggested, it would spoil their favorite outdoor eating spot.

"We are the owners of a fifteen-million-dollar property and because of this proposed upgrade, costing approximately eight-hundred-thousand dollars, we're not only improving the value of our house, but of the entire neighborhood as well. Everyone benefits, it's a win-win. We're conforming to every city building code, and," he turned slightly toward Tom, "we're improving the Parker's property by pruning their neglected landscape at our expense."

Tom hobbled back to his seat as the chairman asked, "Any other comments?"

Silence.

"Then we shall take a vote. All in favor of the project say aye."

There were four loud "Ayes."

"Any against?"

Silence.

"Project approved as presented." The gavel came down and the chairman said, "Next project."

Agnes and Tom were stunned, and then Agnes began to cry quietly, tears running down her cheeks. Her hands trembled as she dabbed at her eyes with a handkerchief. Tom took her hand.

"Come, my darling, let's go home," Tom said softly. "I'm not feeling well." As he reached for Agnes's arm, he faltered. She took his other hand, attempting to help him up.

"Agnes, help me," he now whispered, clutching at his shoulder, then at his chest and his arm. "The pain...it's terrible, help me!" Agnes pulled the bottle of Valium from her handbag and placed a pill in Tom's mouth.

"Swallow it, Tom, it will help you," she urged.

The security guard, who had been standing near the door, walked up the aisle, moved Agnes aside, and eased Tom down across two chairs.

"I'm calling an ambulance," he said as he quickly walked out of the room.

Agnes realized one of the commissioners had stopped talking. The chairman rapped his gavel and announced, "Meeting adjourned."

People began rising from their seats. Walking past Tom, they saw him clutching his chest and making loud moaning sounds. Agnes was on her knees with her hand under Tom's head, her face next to his. "Tom, you're going to be okay," she whispered. "Please Tom, please don't leave me."

Security was ushering people out of the meeting room. As the Harringtons and their entourage passed her, Agnes heard George say to Vivica, "Whew, I'm glad he waited until we were approved."

Vivica smiled and said, "Georgie, you're so bad." Agnes saw Vivica poke George with her elbow and laugh.

Agnes stared at the door. Resentment, anger, bitterness, hatred, these were new feelings for her. When Agnes heard the ambulance, she knew it was real. "Please no, please no," she whispered to herself.

The siren stopped, and she numbly followed the paramedics wheeling Tom on a gurney out of the City Council chambers.

She felt the firm hands of one of the medics, a tall young woman with a ponytail and black boots, helping her up onto a padded bench next to her husband in the ambulance. As the ambulance sped through the traffic lights on Peninsula Road toward the hospital, Agnes leaned over, her face close to her husband's ear, and kept whispering, "Tom, don't leave me...don't leave me...don't leave me," trying to drown out the wail of the siren.

The ambulance slowed and stopped. Abrupt silence; then the harsh glare of lights as the doors opened and two white-coated young men appeared, helped the paramedics pull the gurney out, and then quickly rolled Tom into the emergency entrance. The girl with the ponytail and boots helped Agnes down the ramp and into the hospital where Tom, her husband of almost fifty years, was pronounced dead on arrival.

That night, Agnes returned to the house from the hospital alone, missing Tom terribly. She lay in bed with her eyes open, unable to sleep until the early morning hours when she was awakened by a loud roaring engine noise repeating itself over and over. She lay still, not knowing what the noise could be about.

Walking to the window, she looked out to see an immense yellow bulldozer with an enormous forked scoop repeatedly going forward and backward next to the two tall pine trees on the adjacent property. Agnes was transfixed as she watched the trees lean and then fall with a deafening crash. She stood there for a long time wondering how this could be happening so fast. The pool house had only been approved the night before.

She dressed and decided to go next door and plead for them to wait, to give her time for some quiet mourning. As she walked outside, she saw trucks parked on both sides of the street, with workmen carrying equipment out of the trucks.

She started to walk over to the Harringtons' just as George Harrington emerged from the house toward her with two suitcases and several backpacks. He handed the suitcases to the men who were loading a moving van.

"Excuse me, Mr. Harrington, but I don't know if you know that my dear husband passed away last night," Agnes began. "So, I was thinking that maybe you could wait just a little bit with your construction so I could have some quiet time to grieve."

"Gosh, I'm so sorry, Ms. Parker, but I'm under the wire, time-wise, to get our things into the moving van."

"You know, there is going to be a lot of noise and chaos until construction is finished, so we rented a condo in Marin for a few months." He paused. "I think you might want to do that, too."

Agnes stood there, dumbfounded.

"We are really sorry, but we cannot delay anything now, it would cost a fortune," George continued as he unlocked his car door.

"Have a great day, Ms. Parker!" he said, as he got into his car and drove off.

Three days later, Agnes sat in the funeral home with her sister Louise waiting for Tom's casket to be brought in from the reposing room. The sisters were quiet and held hands like they used to when they were children. Agnes had never been sadder; Tom's funeral was the next afternoon.

They heard the wide doors of the funeral chapel open and watched as two men wheeled Tom's casket down the aisle. Agnes walked to the casket. She looked down at Tom and thought he had never looked more handsome. She placed her hands over his and thought back to the morning several weeks before, when he had brought coffee and the Chronicle back to their bed as he had been doing since retirement. He took the sports section and Agnes read the movies and entertainment as they drank their coffee. They talked about how fast time had passed, and of the new neighbors who had changed everything on the once-quiet island.

Agnes had asked Tom what he thought about the idea of having a fiftieth anniversary party. They agreed that it would be great fun and looked forward to planning it. They kissed and got up to begin their daily routines.

Part 2

After the funeral, Agnes tried to return to life as it was before Tom's death. She often sat outside in the late afternoons after the Harringtons' construction workers had gone and thought about her life with Tom. She would close her eyes and think of his face as he would tell their friends how he felt his heart stop when he first saw Agnes when they were still in high school.

They had married shortly after finishing their undergraduate degrees in college. Agnes recreated in her mind the happy years she'd worked as a receptionist in a law firm supporting Tom through his Ph.D. He was so determined to become a professor.

At night, in order to fall asleep, she would practice the relaxation and meditation they started doing together when they learned of Tom's heart condition. When she ate, she remembered the cooking classes she took to learn how to prepare heart-healthy meals. When she did her volunteer work at the animal shelter, she thought of how she and Tom had acquired their first dog on the advice of their heart doctor and how this had started Agnes's devotion to animal rescue.

Every day she awoke to hammering and pounding interspersed with the loud conversations of the workmen. She tried to resume her normal activities: volunteering, lunch with friends, and attending lectures at her club. It was symphony season and she invited individual friends to join her using Tom's ticket.

When her book group arrived at her house the following month for their scheduled afternoon meeting, the screaming electric saws and pounding hammers made it impossible for their discussion, so they made another date at another member's house to discuss the scheduled book.

After the book group members left, Agnes went to her bedroom, got into bed, and cried. She felt very angry at the Harringtons, especially for what they'd said about Tom when they walked past her at the hearing. She hated them for what she believed they'd done to her husband.

A week later, she knew she could no longer continue her life as it had been. She was going to have to make a change. She packed some clothing, her make-up and other personal items, and moved in with her sister, Louise, not too far away in San Francisco.

Agnes seemed to be adjusting, but about a week after she'd moved in with Louise, she turned to her sister and said, "Louise, I just feel terribly unhappy. I miss Tom so. I miss our house and our beautiful view. And I can't stop thinking, how could they have done that to us? I know it was all legal, but it was not *moral* and it was so unkind. I am still feeling very angry at the Harringtons."

She paused. "I just can't stop thinking about it. I think about it when I wake up, when we go for walks, when I try to sleep at night."

Agnes's energy was gone. When Tom died it seemed her good life went with him. All the things she had always loved: movies, theater, the symphony, her work with rescue animals, visiting with friends, even reading. She dropped out of the book group she'd belonged to for thirty years. She did join a bereavement group, but after three meetings, she refused to attend any more.

One day at breakfast, she stopped eating, and said, "Louise, I have become obsessed with the Harringtons. I am convinced they caused Tom's death and ruined my life."

"Agnes, Tom was seventy-four, and you know he had a heart condition," Louise responded, gently. "It was quite possibly coincidental that he passed away at the meeting."

Agnes would not listen. "Louise, I'm convinced that the stress of that meeting caused his death." She paused. "And this is even harder for me to tell you, but I've lost interest in living except for, and this is very disturbing to me, this new feeling of hatred that is filling all my thoughts. I want revenge."

Her sister put her arms around Agnes. "Agnes, we both know that as time passes, the hurt will lessen. We just have to give it more time. Let's wait a little longer, and then if you still feel this way, you might consider some kind of therapy. I have actually been seeing someone I would like you to meet."

"Seeing someone? What do you mean?"

"Okay, Agnes, I've been seeing a witch!"

"A witch?" Agnes stared at her sister. "What do you mean, a witch? I always knew you were a little weird, but, a *witch*?"

"Yes! It's true. After I retired I was feeling depressed, but I didn't want to worry you, so I never said anything. Anyway, my neighbor across the hall referred me to this woman who claims to be a witch. I've been seeing her weekly, and I look forward to our visits. I have a lot of faith in her. She is intuitive, and really has the ability to make you feel better. She worships nature and believes that the world and everything in it was created by both a God and a Goddess. Agnes, she can create spells; she knows when people are good and when they are bad. Her name is Wyndsong."

"Louise, I don't want to wait," said Agnes, taking in this stream of information. "I want to see her now. I'm just too sad to wait any longer."

Louise called Wyndsong, who said they could come right over, and a few minutes later Louise was ringing the bell next to Wyndsong's black painted door, which was opened by a tall, slender, middle-aged woman with long dark hair and bright blue eyes.

"Please come in," she said. Agnes and Louise walked into a narrow hallway with soft, low lighting illuminating pale gray walls.

"Louise, how nice to see you, as always. This must be your sister, Agnes," she said, taking Agnes's hand in hers and holding it for a moment.

"My name is Wyndsong," the woman told Agnes. "Your sister has told me about your troubles and how sad and angry you are. I'm going to help you feel better," she said reassuringly.

Listening to Wyndsong's soft voice and looking into her blue eyes had a relaxing effect on Agnes. As they walked down the hall, Agnes was mesmerized by the graceful way that Wyndsong moved and how her long silky dress clung and then fell away from her body. They walked to a door on the left and entered a large dimly lit room.

As Agnes stepped into the room, she slipped off her shoes as Wyndsong and Louise had done before her, and felt the soft, pale-colored carpeting under her feet. She inhaled the lavender scent from the candles burning on low glass tables. The room's two large windows were covered in sheer, pale gray curtains, which glided along with the movement around them. Three chairs with gray seat and back cushions sat next to a round table that was covered to the floor in a pale gray cloth. At the center of the table was a small, clear, crystal ball.

Wyndsong motioned for the sisters to sit on either side of her, taking hold of Agnes's left hand and Louise's right. In her soft, melodious voice, Wyndsong asked them to close their eyes and breathe, relax, and feel the peace in the room. Agnes felt calm for the first time since Tom had passed away. She felt warm and secure, her body softening and drifting as she heard Wyndsong's soft voice say, "Now, open your eyes and gaze into the crystal."

Agnes gazed into the crystal ball. At first she saw nothing but the beautiful clear round crystal. Then the crystal swirled, and it looked like there were images forming, coming and going, when suddenly there appeared a clear vision of the Harringtons, the people who had caused all her sorrow. They were seated around a long table outdoors, next to their new pool house: the four beautiful, young, tow-headed children, the handsome parents, four gray-haired older people, all of them eating, talking, laughing.

Agnes felt herself falling. The next thing she knew, Wyndsong and Louise were rubbing her back and speaking in low tones.

"Are you okay?" Louise asked Agnes.

"Yes, I think so," Agnes replied, a bit confused. "But I saw them, Louise. The Harringtons were sitting outside in the garden at their table with their family having a wonderful time." She began to cry.

Wyndsong stroked her hand and said, "Agnes, there is something called Divine Retribution. At our next meeting, we will call Nemesis, the Goddess of Retribution, and appeal to her to bring pain to those who have done this evil to you."

For the first time in months, Agnes felt a sense of calm. She wanted to bring pain to the Harringtons, and she now knew that Wyndsong could help her make the Harringtons suffer like she and Tom had suffered. She could not forget how they had joked about Tom's death at the Council meeting.

She and Louise talked the next day at breakfast.

"Agnes, you have to be really sure that this is what you want because Wyndsong does have the power to bring unhappiness to those who have been cruel and have wronged others."

"I'm definitely ready to visit Wyndsong again," said Agnes. "I know it sounds strange but from the first moment I met her, I began feeling very calm, even happy. I know she can help me through this. I have a tremendous urge to *do* something, Louise, and I believe Wyndsong knows what that something is. I feel like she's someone I've known for a long time and that she can take away my pain."

Louise called Wyndsong, and the next day, the sisters again

went to see her.

As they entered the apartment, Agnes was aware again of the soft, low lighting and the candles casting shadows on the walls. The curtains danced a slow ballet with the breeze from an open window. On the round table sat the shimmering crystal ball. Agnes counted nine small, flickering candles in clear crystal holders surrounding the ball. On a small glass plate next to the crystal ball were three beautifully-shaped white dinner rolls, their tops softly browned.

When she saw Agnes looking at the rolls, Wyndsong explained that simple aromatic bread helps attract the spirits who may still seek physical nourishment. The candles, she said, were for those spirits who seek warmth and light. Agnes could feel her bare feet root into the soft carpet, and she relaxed into the utter and total quiet that surrounded her.

Wyndsong gently took Agnes's hand and guided her to one of the three chairs arranged around the table. Agnes sank into the soft cushions of her chair with contentment and anticipation. Wyndsong and Louise sat on either side of her.

Wyndsong said, "Let us join hands and summon the Goddess Nemesis. Together let us say: Our beloved Nemesis, we bring you gifts from life. Commune with us, Nemesis, and move among us."

There was utter silence in the room. They repeated their request twice more. Agnes watched the crystal ball begin to swirl and soon a figure appeared: a woman with somber eyes and a halo of curly dark hair; arms moving about, swirling and blurry, and then becoming clear.

Wyndsong now said softly, "Beloved Nemesis, we want to bring great harm to the people who have been so insensitive and cruel to the kind and gentle Parkers."

Agnes saw Nemesis sway and move and melt and then after what seemed to be several minutes, the image of the Harringtons appeared clearly before her. Agnes felt warm and buoyant, as though she were floating on water. Her eyelids were heavy and she could no longer keep her eyes open.

Wyndsong said softly, "Agnes, visualize great harm coming to that family. Concentrate, think very hard."

Agnes felt Wyndsong grip her hand. "Agnes, concentrate, focus, think very hard. You are going to cause harm to come to the Harringtons."

And then Wyndsong said, "Powers of darkness, make this so."

Agnes stared at the crystal ball until Nemesis appeared, first wavy and twirling and then well-defined and clear. Next to her was the hated pool house. Agnes's heart began to pound as she recognized the Harringtons' two blonde children, one a small boy, the other a girl of about ten, run out of the pool house and around the pool. The girl said, "Bobby, come on, Mommy's leaving, we are never coming back here. She says she hates it here!"

The boy started to cry, and said, "I like it here, I don't want to go. I want to stay with Dad."

The girl ran up the stairs to the big house.

Agnes watched as the little boy followed her, but then tripped and fell backward, where he lay motionless at the bottom of the stairs. Then the image began fading, swirling gray colors materializing in the crystal ball, and Nemesis appeared again. Soon she was replaced by another image.

This time Agnes saw a courtroom. Above the door leading into the room was the sign "Bankruptcy Court." At the long table in front of the judge, Agnes saw handsome George Harrington, elbows on the table, holding up his head, and beside him another man, standing and speaking to the judge. Soon, that image began to fade, and then blackness.

Agnes woke with her arms on the table, her head resting on her arms. Both Wyndsong and Louise were rubbing her back and asking if she was okay.

"Tell us what happened," Wyndsong said.

Agnes sat very quietly for quite a while and then said softly,

"I wished for the Harringtons' unhappiness" She started to cry. "I saw them arguing, fighting. I saw the children so sad and the little boy falling down the stairs. I saw a court, a bankruptcy court..." Agnes covered her face and cried.

Agnes stayed in bed for several days after the meeting with Wyndsong. Every day, Louise tapped gently on her bedroom door, and when Agnes didn't answer, she would go into the room, where it looked as if Agnes was sleeping.

Finally, on the fourth day, Louise touched Agnes's shoulder very gently and said, "Agnes, Agnes, wake up. I'm very worried about you. You haven't eaten anything for days."

Agnes opened her eyes and looked at Louise.

Louise sat down on the bed and asked, "Agnes, what are you feeling? What are you thinking about?"

"Louise, I feel so bad about what I've seen and what I may have done. I'm ready to go back home and resume my life." She paused and said, "The children are innocent, and after I saw what I wished for in the crystal ball, I realized that I don't want any of it to happen."

She was quiet for a moment, then got up and out of bed. "Louise, please help me pack. I want to go back home." But when most of her things were packed, Agnes again started feeling depressed and hopeless.

Louise told her she could stay as long as she wanted and tried to cheer her up. "Agnes, you know that everything we did with Wyndsong was actually just to make you feel better. In reality, you can't just wish for things to happen."

The next day, Agnes came into the kitchen where her sister was washing the dishes. "Louise, I can't sleep, I can't eat, and I can't read," she told her sister. "I simply don't want to live anymore."

And a week later Agnes passed away.

Louise felt sad and lonely after Agnes died. She told herself that time is a great healer, and that she had already gotten through a lot of deaths. She tried to remember them all:

Grandma Ada and Grandma Minnie, Grandpa Sam and Grandpa Abe, Daddy and Mother, her favorite Uncle Meyer, and Uncle Sam, Auntie Evelyn, and Aunt Bernice. Then she thought of so many of her longtime friends, and now, her only sister, Agnes.

Wyndsong called Louise two weeks after Agnes's funeral.

"Louise dear, are you going to be home this afternoon? I would like to come and visit. My sister has been visiting and she made a batch of her famous peanut butter cookies that I want to share with you."

"You are so nice," Louise responded. "It would be wonderful to see you."

When Wyndsong arrived, Louise stepped out into the garden to greet her with a big hug. "I am so sorry about Agnes," Wyndsong said. "She was such a good person. I know you must miss her a great deal."

"Yes," Louise replied. "I don't really understand why, but I guess it was just her time to go." Wyndsong handed Louise the box of cookies.

"Wyndsong, thank you so much. Let's go inside and I'll make us some tea."

The two women sat in Louise's comfortable living room eating cookies and drinking tea.

They talked about local events, mostly about how things on Deer Island had changed due to all the new people.

Louise picked up some newspaper clippings from the coffee table that had been torn from the *Bay Area Gazette*. Hands trembling, she gave one to Wyndsong, asking, "Have you seen this? It happened two weeks ago, right after Agnes passed away."

Wyndsong looked at the article:

VENTURE PARTNERS OUST CEO GEORGE HARRINGTON

George Harrington, thirty-six, was fired by the Board of Directors of Venture Partners. It was reported that undisclosed expenditures...

Wyndsong looked up as Louise handed her another page.

"This was a week ago," Louise said as she began to cry.

A memorial service is planned for George Harrington, who committed suicide shortly after being fired from his role as CEO of the large firm Venture Partners...

"How sad," Wyndsong said. "Is that the same family that lived next to your sister Agnes?" Louise nodded as she looked at Wyndsong, who was dabbing at her eyes with a handkerchief.

"Louise, these are just terrible coincidences," Wyndsong said. "I think that after being fired for dishonesty, suicide is not so surprising. Try not to think about it, certainly not that you or Agnes were responsible for this. Now please, you need to rest. What do you think about a nap? I always feel so refreshed after an afternoon nap."

Wyndsong walked into the bedroom with Louise and sat next to her as she slipped off her shoes and lay down on the bed.

"Louise, I know how hard it is, but it is best to let go of the past and just move on."

"Wyndsong, I know you're right. I do need to move on," Louise said, taking Wyndsong's hand.

"I'm glad you agree," Wyndsong said, getting ready to leave. She leaned over and gave Louise a hug. "Remember, Louise, there are never really any endings, happy or otherwise. Life just goes on."

DESTINY

Friday, August 6th — 5:30am

Marya turned over and stretched before she opened her eyes to look at the alarm clock. Great, she thought, another half hour of rest on this momentous Friday. She snuggled up to her husband Michael and began to run her fingers across his back. He took her hand.

"Honey, let me sleep," he mumbled. "Got the whole weekend starting tomorrow."

"How about starting now in bed, sweetheart." She moved her hand lower.

"Hey, give a guy a break, will ya?"

"You used to be a sexy beast in the morning."

"Still am, but more on weekends, okay?" He rolled away.

Marya put her arms around him and felt a little sad as she remembered back to when their relationship was new and how eager Michael always was to make love with her. She fell back to sleep until the alarm awakened them both.

Michael rolled over and kissed her.

"Morning, baby, love you."

"I love you, too."

She kissed him on the cheek and slid out of bed, enjoying the feel of her feet on the thick, soft carpet. She walked into her bathroom and, as always, reveled in her surroundings. She loved the tiles from Portugal, the full-length mirrors, her Jacuzzi bath. How lucky she was to live in such a beautiful house.

She brushed her teeth, washed her face, and put on her running clothes. She could hear Michael singing in his shower as she went down the stairs.

Marya entered the kitchen and saw Suzie, their black Lab, step out of her doggie bed, stretch, then bound across the kitchen, tail wagging, to greet her.

"Hi, pretty girl, ready for our morning run?"

Marya bent over and scratched Suzie's back, and Suzie gave Marya a big lick-kiss on her cheek in return. Marya took her running shoes out of their cabinet in the laundry room, sat down, and put them on while Suzie sat at the door, waiting for her.

"Come, we have to say goodbye to your dad." Suzie followed her into the hallway, and Marya called upstairs. "Michael, honey, I'm going on my run..."

"Wait, let me kiss you goodbye," he called down to her. "I'm catching the 7:20 into the city and won't be here when you get back."

He came down the stairs, greeted Suzie, and put his arms around Marya. "I'm sorry about this morning — you know I love to make love with you. I'll make it up tomorrow — we'll have a double-hitter!"

He kissed her and she kissed him back. "It's okay sweetheart — tomorrow we might just stay in bed all day," she laughed. "Remember about my meeting this afternoon. I'm soon going to be rich and free!"

"I do darling — and I know it will go spectacularly well!"

She backed away slightly and looked into Michael's eyes.

"I love you so much!"

"I love you, too. You're beautiful, you know that?"

"What about breakfast?"

"I'll pick up something at the station."

"Oh, Michael, please don't get those really sugary cinnamon rolls — they're a heart attack waiting to happen — so not good for you."

"Don't worry, baby. You make me eat so healthy all the time, a slip once in a while can't possibly hurt!"

She laughed. "Okay, see you tonight. Seven o'clock at the Four Seasons. We have reservations. It's Alice's birthday besides my celebration."

"I know, I know. There'll be six of us — the Stones and the

Blakes," he said as he ran back upstairs.

She began to think about what she was going to wear that night but was interrupted by Suzie's nuzzling her hand.

"Okay, Suzie, we're going!"

She and Suzie went out the door, down the driveway, and into the street where they ran to meet Marya's long–time running mate, Alice Stone, jogging toward them from down the block.

"Hello beautiful girl!" Alice said, hugging Suzie as the dog jumped up to greet her.

"Hi Alice, happy birthday!" said Marya.

"Thanks. Thirty-seven. I can't believe it, Marya. Closer to forty than thirty...I'm getting old too fast!"

"Excuse me, but you do know how old I am, right?"

"Sorry, I know I should respect my elders!"

"I may be older than you but I'm still a faster jogger and I always will be, even when we're in our seventies. And don't forget it, birthday girl."

The two women fell into unison jogging at the same pace, Suzie running alongside, weaving in and out, sometimes ahead, sometimes behind the two women.

"So," began Alice, "you nervous about closing the deal today?"

"Kind of, but no, not really, I'll be happy to finalize it. It's been a very long year-and-a-half — I thought it would never actually happen. So, besides your birthday, we'll be celebrating the sale tonight as well."

"Marya, aren't you also a little sad? I remember when you started that company. You've put a lot more than a lot into it."

"I know, but it's time. Seven years, and you know what they say about everything having a season. I feel that I'm done, and besides, I have a new business idea."

"Oh, tell me."

"I don't want to talk about it before this deal closes. Bad luck. I'll tell you about it tonight."

"Okay, I can wait. So, what are you wearing tonight? Dressy or..."

They chatted as usual as they turned and jogged into the neighborhood park and along the running path. Just past the first curve, Alice stopped.

"Marya, look at that giant boulder, it's bigger than we are. Have you seen that before?"

Marya jogged back to Alice. "Suzie, come," she said to the dog, "we're going back." Suzie came bounding back to where Marya and Alice were now standing.

"Seen what?" Marya asked Alice.

Alice pointed at what looked like the top of a gray boulder, materializing through some recently pruned shrubbery. The two women stood still.

"Oh my God, Alice, no, I haven't noticed that before. What is it?"

Suzie following, both women walked off the path into the park toward a large boulder, barely visible through the greenery. Alice leaned over and moved some branches away so they could see the flat face of the boulder. They stood together and read the words carved into the stone:

SOMETIMES DEATH COMES UNANNOUNCED
WITH NO TIME FOR EVEN A BRIEF FAREWELL
SARAH ELIZABET NEWCOMB
AUGUST 24, 1856 – JULY 18, 1892

They looked at each other. "Wow, only thirty-six. That's really sad," Marya said. "Around our age, way too young to die. I wonder," she went on, "why we never noticed it before?"

"It's probably because they've done a lot of pruning here in the park. Or maybe it's because we're always too busy exercising our tongues while we exercise our bodies!" said Alice.

"Okay, let's get a move on," said Marya, checking her watch.

"Suzie, come, let's go." They both smiled as Suzie ran past them, and they began jogging again.

"I wonder who Sarah Elizabet was," Alice said.

"Let's see who remembers to Google her," Alice replied.

Marya returned home at seven-thirty and went upstairs to shower and get dressed for her important meeting that afternoon. She took extra time to select her business attire plus what she would take with her to change into for that night. Her make-up also took longer because she wanted to look her best for the big meeting with her lawyers and H. B. Myers, the company committed to buying the online business she had created — At Your Service, an online concierge service that had caught on and grown beyond her original dream.

She was still in wonder that no one else had thought of it. She'd created it because she herself had needed someone to pick up groceries, the dry cleaning, buy theater tickets, organize plane tickets, find someone to clean the house, help at parties. Really, it was such an obvious idea.

Of course, now there were several copycats, but she had been the first, the original, and that was what H. B. Myers was buying. She felt excited. It had been a long year-and-a-half of non-stop focus and negotiating and finally it was going to happen. And yes, Alice was right, she felt a little sadness too — it's hard to give up "a child."

Marya looked closely into her dressing-table mirror. Was she seeing lines around her eyes? And were there suddenly more gray hairs than yesterday? She was forty-one and had spent the last seven years building At Your Service. It was tough, first perfecting the model, fine-tuning it, making it work. Then she'd had to convince the venture capitalists of her concept's potential viability in order to get financing to grow. She'd had to hire the executives the VCs said were needed in order to run her company, and then realized how naive she'd been when it came to corporate machinations.

How unhappy Marya had been the last two years. As

instructed by the VCs, she had hired seasoned executives from big Internet companies: a CEO and a CFO with lots of experience. But it was hard for her to just hand over her "baby," which she had created, nurtured, stayed up with at night, thought about every day, gave preference to over husband and self, all the time knowing that it was she who knew what was best for her own creation.

Then, having to go along with changes she did not believe were the right thing, not being able to do what she wanted, always needing to have the approval of the board, the VCs and Senior Executives.

How lucky for her that H. B. Myers had come into the picture. They saw the beauty of her brainchild and wanted to acquire it. How fortunate that she was able to convince the Board to go along with the sale when all five of them were skeptical. She smiled. She had always known she had Lady Luck on her shoulder.

And today she would see the tangible proof of that. After today, she'd be freed up and could start living each day exactly how she wanted to instead of for the day her company would be sold. She smiled at herself in the mirror, picked up the dress, shoes and handbag she had chosen for dinner that night and ran down the stairs.

As she entered the kitchen, Suzie came to greet her. Marya scratched behind the dog's ears and gave her a hug. How happy Suzie always was just to see Michael and her — maybe they would take her to the dog park tomorrow. They all had such a good time there.

She fed Suzie, and had her own usual breakfast of juice, fruit, yogurt, and herbal tea. She scanned the local *Sun Times* headlines and looked quickly at the business section to see what companies were being acquired and if there was anything about her company. She scanned Nancy Graham and Tom Moseley's columns, her two favorites — Nancy for her news about who went to what event with whom, and what they wore; Tom for his witty take on what was happening in city government.

She glanced at her watch, then put her spoon, bowl, cup, and glass into the dishwasher and dialed the dog sitter.

"Hi, Loraine. You haven't forgotten about us today, have you? Oh, okay, see you in five. Also, can you bring Suzie home tonight? We're going out to dinner directly after work, so I won't be able to pick her up. I'll leave the key in the usual place. Super. Thanks."

She hung up and told Suzie that Loraine would be here soon, put on Suzie's leash, grabbed her handbag, briefcase, and extra outfit, and took Suzie out the front door to wait.

Loraine's van pulled up in front of the house as promised and Suzie ran to greet Loraine. Marya pulled the van door open.

"Hi Loraine, Suzie is always so happy to see you."

"Thanks," she said. "Likewise."

Suzie jumped in and Marya slid the door closed, then watched the van drive away. As she watched the van disappear down the street, Marya already missed Suzie and pushed away the thought that she was already nine, fairly old for a dog. Marya and Michael were both so involved in their careers and had decided against having a family, so Suzie was really like their child.

Marya was about to walk to her car in the driveway when she heard the phone ring inside the house. She hesitated. Should she go back into the house and answer or not? She decided to check voicemail from her cell and walked to her car.

Once on the freeway, she turned on her favorite talk radio host, Bryce Vernon. From a distance, she saw an enormous truck loaded with boulders turn up onto the Concord Dam overpass. She picked up her cell and called her home voicemail. The call was from her mother, and she smiled in anticipation of the message.

"Hello dear, just wanted to remind you to call me after the meeting today, I'll be thinking positive th..."

Marya heard a loud rumbling from above.

Friday, August 6th — 1:30pm

Michael walked rapidly down the hallway back to his office, pleased at how the meeting had gone. These people were potentially very big clients, and if they decided to go with the firm, there was a good chance that he'd be made a partner.

His thoughts were interrupted by Christina, the office receptionist, who was walking toward him.

"Michael, there are two policemen here who want to talk to you."

Michael followed Christina out to the reception area where indeed there were two uniformed Highway Patrol officers.

"How can I help you?" Michael asked.

They both handed him their ID's and he glanced at their names.

"Sir," said the tall patrolman on the left, "we would like to talk to you privately if we can."

"Can you tell me what this is about?" Michael felt a twinge. He wondered, *Did they catch me speeding on radar or what?*

"Sir, we need to speak with you privately."

He felt reluctant. He didn't want to speak with them, but said,

"Okay, sure, just follow me..."

Michael felt his heart begin to beat a little faster. What was this about?

They entered Michael's office, and stood facing one another.

"Please sit down, sir," the tall one spoke quietly. "We are going to have to tell you some bad news."

Michael walked around his desk and sat down, looking at the two patrolmen. He nodded toward the chairs in front of his desk and said, "Please sit down."

The tall patrolman took out a notebook from his jacket pocket.

"You are Michael Godard, Marya Bennett's husband," he paused, "that is correct?"

Michael could feel his heart beginning to pound in his chest; he was beginning to feel sick. He nodded, "Yes?"

"We are very sorry to inform you, sir, that at approximately 9:45 AM this morning, on the 103 South, there was an accident..."

Saturday, August 7th

SUN TIMES

WOMAN DIES IN FREAK ACCIDENT
BY CHARLIE GOODWIN,
***SUN TIMES* STAFF WRITER**

ON FRIDAY MORNING AT 9:45 A TRUCK LOADED WITH QUARRY ROCK BOUND FROM WINSTON TO THE CONCORD DAM CONSTRUCTION SITE OVERTURNED ONTO THE FREEWAY BELOW FROM THE 586 OVERPASS, CRUSHING THE AUTO DRIVEN BY MARYA BENNETT, 41, KILLING HER INSTANTLY. SOUTHBOUND TRAFFIC WAS HALTED FOR HOURS AS AUTHORITIES . . .

THE HUNT

PART I: 1990 - A HOUSE ON DEER

Steve Wolfe, a tall, handsome, twenty-six-year-old MIT grad and founder of logistic-artisans.com, and his beautiful, blonde, twenty-four-year-old wife, Frances, were visiting Steve's former college friend, Rick Collins, who was staying with his parents on Deer Island, a suburb of San Francisco.

Steve and Frances drove down a long boulevard to Golden Gate Avenue, a single circular street that leads both on and off the relatively small island, which has only 982 houses and a handful of shops. It was early afternoon on a quiet Saturday. They were silent as they drove up Golden Gate past the carefully tended gardens visible only through the high iron gates in the walls surrounding each house. Arriving at the end of Golden Gate, the tallest point on the island, they parked and got out of their new Maserati.

They stood, enthralled with the view across the bay.

"Steve, you can see the city from here!" Frances said.

"And the bay and all three bridges," Steve added. "And I've heard it's only twenty minutes to the city by ferry."

He put his arm around his wife's narrow waist.

"What would you think of buying a house here on Deer Island and leaving the condo behind?"

"Awesome," she replied.

They drove back down to the address on Belvedere Avenue to meet Rick. The Wolfes' tall, blonde friend answered the door of his parents' home.

"Welcome to Paradise," Rick said. "My folks bought this house when they retired ten years ago. Not a bad place to live, right?"

Rick's parents were surprised when the Wolfes announced their intention to buy a house on Deer at dinner that evening.

Discussing their plans, Rick's dad told the Wolfes that they would probably be the youngest homeowners on the island.

"This has been an ideal place for seniors like us to retire," he said.

"Maybe we'll start a trend," Steve laughed. "We've been pretty good at that, you know."

The next morning, the Wolfes and Rick went for a walk around the small island, and that afternoon Rick Senior introduced them to the only realtor on Deer, Nora Taylor, elegant in a black pantsuit and white silk shirt. A slender woman in her fifties, she exuded energy, her make-up and hair impeccably done.

"Welcome to Deer," she said, handing them each her business card as Rick Senior took his leave.

"I've been selling real estate here on the island for twenty years and it is a wonderful place to live," Nora went on, then paused, as if making a difficult mental calculation.

"There aren't many houses for sale on the island, so I'm hoping we have what you're looking for." She paused, then asked, "What price range?"

"Frances," Steve said, looking at his wife, "do you have anything particular in mind?" When she shook her head no, Steve continued, "I think location-wise we want something near the top of the island with a view of the city."

"Okay," replied Nora. "How many bedrooms?"

"Oh, we don't care about the house," Steve interrupted. "The view is what we want."

"All right, then, what price range?" Nora asked again with slightly raised eyebrows. Turning to his wife, Steve asked,

"What do you think, Frances?"

She shrugged her shoulders, "Whatever you think, honey."

Turning back to Nora, Steve said, "How about one to ten?"

Nora shook her head. "Oh, I'm afraid there's nothing for a hundred thousand, you..."

Steve stopped her short, "No, Nora, one to ten million."

True to Nora's heads up, there were not many houses for sale on Deer. Nora drove Steve and Frances slowly around the island, stopping to show them the five larger homes that were available. None of them, however, had an unobstructed view of the city skyline. Standing with Frances next to Nora after their final walk-through, Steve spotted a large, white mansion at the highest point of the island.

"There!" Steve insisted, "That's the house we want!"

"Oh my, that's Deer Villa, a Willis Polk design." Nora seemed flustered.

"Willis Polk," Steve interrupted, "isn't he the famous architect?"

For the first time, Steve seemed genuinely impressed. And so was Nora with her young client. Clearly, Steve was more than a mere techie who had hit it big.

Nora pocketed her car key and led the couple to a path half-hidden from the parked car on the side of the road.

"I think it might be a good idea for us to walk a little, so we can see more," she said, pointing toward Deer Villa, a large three-story white mansion with rows of windows trimmed in the last century's rococo-style trim. Nora went on,

"It was the first house on the island and it is not for sale. It was built about a century ago by a retired physician, Doctor Redmond."

"And the name Deer Island, how did that originate?" Frances asked.

"That's uncertain, but most people today suppose from the small herd of native deer present on the island," Nora said.

"It was Doctor Redmond who founded the Wild Deer Rescue Association, then purchased all the land that wasn't owned by the state, planning to make the entire island a deer sanctuary. No fences and no other houses, just Deer Villa."

"Oh," Frances said, "I love deer."

Nora smiled. "Deer Villa has always belonged to the Redmond family. Doctor Redmond's four granddaughters live there now. They're a little eccentric. Not dangerous, but eccentric," she repeated for emphasis.

"Tell us more, Nora," Steve said, looking at Frances, who nodded and said, "Yes, please go on."

Nora continued, "Over the years, the Redmond family sold most of the lots, and houses were built. Deer is still a quiet place, and with mostly retired people living here, there's practically no crime.

"Awesome," Frances said.

Holding hands, Frances and Steve walked down the street with Nora at their side, seemingly abandoning her car. As they passed a small, forested area, Frances caught sight of three deer gracefully disappearing into the trees.

"Steve," Frances said, "the deer are beautiful. The view of the city is gorgeous. I love watching the seagulls diving for fish. I really want to live here."

Steve glanced at Nora, and then over her shoulder up a narrow one-lane street to a smallish, dark, wood-shingled house. Situated high up on the island, it obviously provided its owners with a magnificent view.

"How about that one?" he ventured, pointing to the property. A white "For Sale" sign was nailed on a post at the curb directly in front of the house.

"We'll take that one, then, I think that's the one we want."

"But isn't that too small?" Nora responded. "It's a one-bedroom summer cottage."

Ignoring her, Steve went on, "And check out the house next door. There's no sign, but see if we can buy that one, too." By the year's end, Steve and Frances had purchased the first two-million-dollar properties ever sold on Deer.

PART II: 2000 – THE WILD DEER

Ten years had passed since the Wolfes made their initial

offers, bulldozed the two houses, and built their mega-mansion. And then, gradually, one by one, the island's well-tended gardens, simple summer houses, and retired seniors disappeared, replaced by new 10,000 square-foot mansions and the young entrepreneurs who owned them.

The Deer's *Globe* newspaper, hub of island communications, published letters to the editor. There was always some bit of new gossip, the latest being that the city of Deer Island was being sued by an outraged new landowner, Peter Donovan, an inventor and owner of the patent on a child's safety seat for cars, whose request to build a 20,000 square-foot house had been denied. He sued, asserting that he'd never give up, that he had more money than the city of Deer, and that he'd continue to sue until he won.

"That's how I got where I am at my young age. *Never give up* is my motto," he said.

Quiet, peaceful Deer was now a thing of the past. Then came the latest news: the deer, once barely in evidence, seemed to be multiplying. They were everywhere — on the streets, in any garden that was not fenced, even in the local park and playground. It was not unusual to see a herd of five or six of them flushed from their habitat near a road, darting out in front of cars before finally disappearing into one of the fewer and fewer traces of forest.

The new citizens of Deer were outraged! A new Deer Island resident wrote in a *Globe* guest editorial that one day as she was walking her dog, she looked behind her and was startled to see a buck with a large rack of antlers following her. Fortunately, the editorial writer went on to say, she was passing an open garage where a contractor was working. The man began shouting at the buck who finally retreated. The woman ended the editorial with the demand that the city take action to defend its citizens from the wild deer.

The local activity and commotion caused by both the invasion of the young *nouveau riche* and the plea to eliminate the deer went largely unnoticed in the house Dr. Redmond had built at the top of the island in 1918. In their sixties and retired from their careers of nursing and school teaching, the four Redmond granddaughters, Evelyn, Helen, Florence, and Margaret, now lived full-time in their grandfather's house with their longtime house-man Joseph and his wife Clara.

The sisters didn't acknowledge the newcomers whom they referred to as "*Johnnie-come-latelies*" and continued to socialize only with the few older residents still remaining. They preferred that Joseph drive them in to San Francisco, where they spent their time volunteering as docents in the museums, or attending the opera, symphony, and theater.

At the monthly meeting of the town council, a deer committee was formed "to address the deer problem. That week's *Globe* introduced the committee members. To no one's surprise, it consisted primarily of the new, more prominent citizens of the island:

Dr. George Johnson, the thirty-four-year-old president of a huge nearby hospital, and best known as the author of a policy requiring proof of US citizenship for any patient before he or she could be treated at the hospital;

Peter Donovan, the thirty-one-year old child safety-seat inventor and entrepreneur;

Dr. Michael Katz, a world-renowned cosmetic surgeon; and of course,

Steve Wolfe, who had started the young, entrepreneurial migration to Deer Island.

If any group could solve the problem, it was this one.

The first meeting took place at Steve and Frances's opulent house. Built on the side of the island facing San Francisco, it sat on a steep slope that eventually led down to the bay. The dramatic entrance to the house began with one wide step down from the street into a glassed-in funicular.

Once inside the house, the view of the ocean, the city, and the bridges was breathtaking. Comfortably cosseted in the soft leather chairs in Steve's home office, the committee members discussed the problem, trying to turn it into a challenge that they could not only meet, but that they could literally make a profit from. Anyone could come up with a plan to eliminate the deer, they opined, but only exceptional individuals such as themselves could turn it into a money-making venture.

The solution the group finally supported originated with Peter. Not only an inventor, Peter was also an avid hunter, having trophies of everything from big game in Africa to alligators and endangered species from South America.

"What," Peter initially ventured, mindful of the huge egos in the room, "would you think of organizing a big-time hunt?"

"What do you mean a hunt?" Michael challenged immediately. "Hunting isn't exactly legal on our island."

George and Steve concurred with some certainty.

As Peter explained, he became more animated, leaning forward in his buttery leather Eames chair.

"Look, with this idea, everybody wins. We organize a unique experience: open season on Deer Island, a once-in-a-lifetime event. But not just for anyone. We advertise it to only the highest rollers. We make it super exclusive; a donation of a million dollars to the charity of the participant's choice will be required," he continued. "As for the law, we'll have it changed...for that one day."

"One million to hunt deer! You're dreaming," Michael said.

"Wait a minute," Peter interrupted. "You don't know these big-time hunters like I do." He then proceeded to launch into stories of his experiences with a Saudi king, the sheikh of Abu Dhabi, the North Korean dictator Kim Jong-il, and the wealthy Chinese official Yang Gong Chun, all of whom Peter had hunted endangered species in the past.

"You have no idea what kind of money people will spend to hunt," Peter said, opening his arms out wide to emphasize *large*.

The room suddenly fell silent. Finally, Michael said, "Okay, let's talk about it."

A lively discussion of Peter's idea and how it might work

ensued, and the more the four men discussed it, the more enthusiastic and excited they each became.

George said, "I'm guessing there are approximately fifty to seventy-five deer on the island with the good news for our hunt being that they are virtually trapped, surrounded by water, with only one way on or off."

"Agreed," said Peter, "and we want to make sure that every hunter bags at least one. So, I think we should limit the event to thirty participants, meaning thirty million dollars for charity, minus expenses. Plus we get rid of the deer at the same time. Brilliant, if I do say so myself."

It was further decided that they would engage the long-time resident Charles Owens, a well-known criminal law attorney, who would represent them in changing the "NO HUNTING" law and any other pesky matters.

Beyond Owens's fee, expenses would be limited to costs for relocating local residents to nearby resorts for the weekend, meals and hotel accommodations for the hunters, the fees for licenses and hunting guides, and of course, whatever it cost to reach out to Peter's select group of hunters.

In the weeks that followed, they talked the hunt up among the locals, and were pleasantly surprised by how little opposition there was.

The plan was written about in the *Globe*, which was where the Redmond sisters first read of the proposal to eliminate the deer.

"You know," said Helen, the oldest sister, "it's bad enough when people hunt deer in remote areas. But here, where they have lived safely and unharmed for decades, it's criminal."

Margaret added, "Hunting deer on an island that bears their name is something we simply cannot allow."

The sisters looked at one another, and proclaimed in unison, "Absolutely not!"

"But what," Helen asked, "can we do about it?"

"We can stage a protest, like people do against war and

explain about Grandfather and the history of the island," said Evelyn.

"You're right, Evelyn, I can't imagine people not being sympathetic," said Helen, looking at her sisters, who nodded in agreement. "Let's plan it for the next council meeting."

They decided to have deer costumes made, which would not only be a surprise to everyone, but would also, they hoped, humanize the deer in a way, bringing sympathy to their cause. They looked forward with excitement to the meeting and to the difference their protest might make.

On the night the city council had set aside to discuss "The Hunt," as it was now being called, the sisters donned the deer costumes that the well-known costume designer Laura Hazlette had created for them, complete with deer-face masks, antlers, and body suits with imitation fur resembling deer hide.

The meeting was to start at six o'clock, and by five, the Redmond sisters were standing in front of city hall in their costumes, handing out colorful leaflets that said SAVE THE DEER ON DEER ISLAND. Below the heading were beautiful photos of the native deer nestled among the trees, jumping high over logs, and one of a mother deer standing guard over adorable twin fawns.

Deer Island residents coming to the meeting were a little shocked as they passed the sisters in their disguises, and could be heard saying, "Who are they?" and "How crazy, whew!" and "Why are they in deer costumes?" and "Where are they even from?

Examining the photos, someone astutely offered, "It looks like they are against deer hunting."

By six o'clock, the meeting room was packed. There were not enough seats and people were standing in the back. The meeting was called to order by the mayor, who introduced the first item on the agenda: THE HUNT.

Just then, the double doors to the room opened and the sisters in their costumes came through, waving their arms and singing in chorus, "Save the deer, save the deer, help us save our deer!"

There was silence in the room as the sisters danced up the aisle toward the stage, where the council members sat, all seemingly shocked. The council president was the first to act; he called security and within seconds, emerging from behind the sisters, two uniformed security guards appeared.

"Sorry," the guards said, as they took hold of the deer impersonators' arms, turned them around, and escorted them toward the door.

Once outside, the short, stocky, blond guard whose name tag identified him as "Ted," said, "This meeting is to decide an important issue; it is open to residents only and you are disrupting the meeting."

The taller guard, Bill, continued, "You are not allowed inside. Residents only. Either wait out here or go back to wherever you came from!"

The guards walked rapidly back into the building and stood, arms folded, their backs in front of the open double doors. Outside, the Redmond sisters took off their masks and Helen and Evelyn began to cry.

"How can this be happening?" asked Helen. "Who are all these new people?"

"We're third-generation Deer residents," Evelyn added through her tears. "They can't do this to us."

"I think it's time we took more drastic steps!" Margaret proclaimed.

The following afternoon, the *Globe* carried a story about the council meeting, once again detailing the plan for eliminating the deer. There was no mention of the Redmond granddaughters' protest. Margaret said, "We need to make a plan."

PART III: THE PLAN

Fortunately, the sisters had time. The Hunt wasn't scheduled to take place for another nine months. It was Helen who suggested they contact the local, state-run Wild Deer Rescue Association, founded by their grandfather with the avowed purpose to conserve, enhance, and promote wild deer throughout the state. The sisters were well known to the organization as they had always generously supported the group.

A day after Helen put in the call, two WDRA rangers, Phil and Dave, arrived at the Redmond home. Evelyn, the oldest of the four sisters, explained the issue, reading aloud from the *Globe*.

"We need you to help us save our deer."

Phil, the older of the two rangers, was immediately sympathetic; lamenting, however, that the Association's hands were tied.

"Look," he said, "Deer Island has been granted a limited license for this hunting event and it would be against the law for us to do anything to help you on the day of the hunt."

"All right," said Evelyn, "we understand. But what if you were to help both parties: the deer and the new residents?"

Phil nodded in response and said, "Nice work if you can get it ladies, but how?"

Evelyn went on to explain. "We have figured out a way to give the residents what they want while at the same time keeping the deer alive."

Phil scratched his head. "Meaning?"

Evelyn continued, "Start gradually relocating the deer from the island, so that there won't be any to hunt. The new residents will be happy about there not being any deer, the deer will be happy to be alive, and the WDRA will be happy about receiving the largest donation the Redmond family has ever contributed at one time: two million dollars."

Phil looked at his partner and said, "Excuse us for a minute," and the two of them left the room. The sisters looked at one another. Florence, the youngest, crossed her fingers and closed her eyes.

The rangers returned shortly. "Okay," Phil started, "we can help, provided there is good cause, and," he added quickly, "there is. Your generous donation will more than help with the expenses of tagging and relocating your deer to a safe place and even returning them when things cool down."

The rangers and the sisters all shook hands, and over the next week papers were drawn up and signed, and the sisters wrote a check for half their promised charitable donation, the other half due upon completion of the assignment. Always considerate of others, the sisters requested the relocation to be done at night so as not to disturb the island's human residents.

And so, it was that several times a week in the early morning hours through the fall and winter between 3:00 and 4:00 AM, the WDRA truck could be seen driving onto Deer Island and shortly thereafter driving off the island with a dozen or more sedated deer inside.

At the same time, a non-profit corporation, Eliminate the Deer, Inc., or ETD, was formed to oversee the execution of Peter's grand plan. Steve, Michael, Peter, and George were installed as corporate officers. They rented an office downtown, on Main Street, hired a local to manage the office, and under the ETD aegis, began contacting Peter's big-game hunting connections.

ETD also arranged with golf and spa resorts within a hundred miles of Deer to accommodate the island's residents for the weekend of the event. They contacted churches and other groups who fed the homeless to find charitable organizations to which they could donate the hundreds of pounds of venison that would result from the hunt to feed the hungry.

"My God," exclaimed Steve, "this is turning out even better than we ever anticipated."

Peter threw his arms skyward and exclaimed loudly, "A total win, win, win!"

As always, George and Michael agreed, the four men toasting the moment with a very fine Veuve Clicquot's Yellow Label Brut.

And so, autumn turned into fall and fall into winter. The sisters were informed weekly on how many deer were being relocated. By February the deed was done with all the Deer Island deer now resident at Reading National Park, where hunting was prohibited.

"Thank you so much for saving our deer," Evelyn said, when Phil phoned with the news. She hung up and looked at her sisters who stood in the hall facing her. All had tears in their eyes.

"You know, said Margaret, "I feel sad and happy at the same time." They hugged each other.

Evelyn was the first to break the scrum. "Okay," she said, "let's plan our big day."

Back on Main Street at EDT, Steve, Michael, Peter, and George had been very busy. In addition to the four of them, they now had four additional people volunteering in the office, helping to organize the big event.

In all, twenty-six prospective hunters had applied to take part, all of whom paid the requisite million dollars for this once-in-a-lifetime event. It was an elite list, all high-profile, well-known individuals, among them, the son of the North Korean Leader Kim Jong-il; six members of the ruling family of Saudi Arabia; a Russian oligarch; the deposed President of Turkey; four high-profile Chinese government officials; and an Arab sheikh, who actually inquired if a million dollars was sufficient to guarantee his place in the hunt.

Team Deer, as the four organizers and four volunteers liked to call themselves, arranged for the entire population of the island, all one thousand, eight hundred and seventy of them, plus their house pets and minus the Redmond sisters, who had refused the offer of relocation, to be transported to their choice of a nearby spa, golf resort, or country club for the weekend.

In addition, the team booked every single room, eighty in all, at the three local hotels to accommodate the hunters and their entourages. This would help ensure the hunters' privacy and further add to the exclusivity of the event.

Beyond the hunt itself, a gala dinner on Saturday night, to be held at the hillside home of Peter Donovan, was a highlight of the event. Team Deer had engaged, at great expense, the world-famous French chef, Jacques Robuchon, to prepare this feast with the *pièce de résistance* being venison, not from the recent kill, but rather well-aged and imported from France, to be accompanied by rare wines, some of which were several hundred dollars a bottle.

Scheduled to attend the dinner were the mayor and other officials of several neighboring cities, the governor of the state, the president of WDRA, a district assemblyman, and several other dignitaries.

Early Friday morning, the private jets began to arrive at the local St. Raymond Private Airport, which had just finished a three-million-dollar renovation in record time in anticipation of the event. Reporters from major American and European newspapers as well as from Russia and the Middle East, were already in downtown Deer interviewing local residents.

The Deer Island police force had enlisted officers from surrounding cities to be on hand the day of the hunt to make sure everything went as planned and that there were no unfortunate incidents. The locals were excited about all the attention they were getting. The story of the unusual event had appeared in many newspapers across the country, and singly or in pairs, Steve, Peter, Michael, and George appeared on NBC's *Meet the Press*, as well as on *Good Morning America*, and the *Today show*.

On Friday, Peter Donovan's opulent home was staged for Saturday's gala dinner, where society editors had been invited for a press conference before the dinner was to begin. A dozen movers in vans removed the furniture from the entire first floor, carefully wrapping each piece and storing it in the van. Next, unmarked trucks appeared and Michael Amini himself organized and placed his custom-built furniture throughout the house.

Twenty-six expert hunting guides had been recruited from Adventure Outfitters, a prestigious, licensed hunting guide group, and early Friday afternoon they began walking the streets and trails of the island to locate small clusters of deer and to map plans for the hunt the next day. After about two hours of searching Deer Island for deer, head guide Robert Corwin broke the increasingly charged silence.

"Hey, what's going on?" said Corwin. "Is this a joke or what? There aren't any deer on this island. There aren't even any signs of them."

After much discussion with his fellow guides, Corwin said, "Look, big hunt, big money, but no deer. Something must be going on, something we don't know. What we do know is that we're all getting paid more than we ever have. So I say, let's let sleeping dogs lie. No use looking for trouble. I would like to suggest that we not say anything."

Several of the other guides shrugged their shoulders, and soon everyone agreed that the guides would say nothing. Later that afternoon, twenty-six limos picked up the hunters at the private airport and brought them to Deer.

Local volunteers were on-hand to help the hunters settle into their hotel rooms. An early Friday night dinner at the trendy new restaurant, Cristiano's, was planned for that evening.

That afternoon, luxury tour buses also were waiting in the local parking lot for the island's residents, who arrived carrying overnight bags and small pets, with larger pets trailing along on leashes. Everyone appeared to be in good spirits. New residents Claire Trevor and her friend Nancy Norris, both interior designers, stood with their bags waiting to get on the bus.

"What a fun event," said Claire. "No one has ever done anything like this before. And it's all for charity."

Nancy responded, "You know, we really are a very special community."

As the entourage of tour buses was leaving Deer, the entourage of limos was arriving. Even though there were only twenty-six hunters, each of them had servants or secretaries, and one of the Saudi princes had brought his personal chef.

Steve, Michael, Peter, George, and the four volunteers were strategically stationed at the three hotels, smiling broadly to greet their guests, whose rooms had each been outfitted with new, luxury cotton towels and robes, the finest goose-down pillows and comforters, and Egyptian cotton 500-thread-count sheets.

At seven o'clock that evening, the hunters were taken to Ristorante Cristiano, where Cristiano himself greeted and welcomed the hunters with a little speech. After a truly superb meal of *stracciatella* and *scampi alla griglia* accompanied by Antinori *Chianti Classico,* the hunters were escorted back to their rooms and told that they would be awakened at five, served a light breakfast, and guided to the deer trails for the hunt, where they would rendezvous with the guides.

In the meantime, Helen, Evelyn, Margaret, and Florence had planned their own Friday morning show. They went over final details that night at dinner.

"Okay, Evelyn, you're going to call Michael at 9:30 tomorrow morning and invite all the hunters and guides up to the house, right?" said Helen.

"Yes, and when they come, what are we going to say first?" asked Margaret, with Florence interrupting, "Should we have our deer costumes on?"

"Yes, of course. The costumes make our point of humanizing our deer and showing that, like us humans, the deer also want to live and enjoy life," said Helen.

"I'm so excited, I can't wait!" exclaimed Florence. She paused and then said, "I think we should be singing and dancing our deer song."

They toasted with their favorite sherry to their anticipated success and retired early to bed.

PART IV: THE HUNT

As promised, the guests were awakened at five in the morning and served a light breakfast. Box lunches were secured in the guides' backpacks, along with the gear for each of their assigned hunters: extra cartridges, binoculars, compasses, snake-bite kits, insect repellant, and first-aid kits, which filled their large backpacks to capacity. The hunters themselves only had small fanny packs and their Deerfield Snipers and Blackhawk Hunters, both considered among the most expensive and lethal of all deer-hunting rifles.

The guides escorted the hunters onto the main island trail. It was 6:00 AM, just sunrise. The sky was orange, the distant mountains dark, silhouetted by the sky and the calm bay, just becoming visible with seagulls screaming and diving for their breakfast.

After a few minutes, the group seemed to quiet down and stood utterly silent; soon the distant sound of a trumpet could be heard, replicating perfectly the start of an English fox hunt.

BaBAAAAAA. BaBAAAAAA.

The hunters and guides began to move and spoke to their entourage in a variety of languages. The guides peered at one another with raised eyebrows. Peter, Michael, Steve, and George trailed behind, at first exuberant, then exchanging questioning looks as it became increasingly apparent that there were no deer to be hunted.

"So, Michael," whispered Steve frantically, "where are they?"

"How the hell should I know?" Michael responded, defensively. "I tried to tell you guys that we hadn't had any complaints lately!"

"Hey," said George, "I just had a thought. What if the deer have actually disappeared?" he joked.

"Don't be an asshole, George," responded Peter.

It was nine-thirty and the group was standing in a large clearing at the top of the island. They looked out at the bay and at San Francisco. They looked in all directions, apparently puzzled, some annoyed and irritated, questioning their guides as to why there were no signs of deer since they had been searching for over three hours.

The Chinese official Yang Gong Chun whispered to his guide in Mandarin, "Who is trying to stop our hunt? In Beijing he would be arrested by now!"

Peter's cell rang.

"Peter, this is Evelyn Redmond calling. How are you?"

"Fine," he replied. "Uh, not really able to talk right now." He paused. "The Hunt, you know."

He put his hand over the phone, whispering to his partners, "It's Evelyn Redmond."

"Sorry to interrupt, but perhaps you all should come up to the house. We have news about your event."

"Let me put you on speaker," Peter said, suddenly subdued. "Can you just say that again?"

Evelyn began to repeat herself when Peter interrupted.

"Look, Evelyn, that's nice of you, but we're in the middle of our big event, we can't..."

"Well, sorry to spoil things for you," she interrupted, "but there are no deer."

Peter held the phone up and looked at the others who seemed frozen where they were.

"What the goddamn hell did you say?" Peter yelled into the phone.

Evelyn calmly repeated, "I said, since you are not going to shoot any deer today, you should come up to the house to find out why..."

Peter touched the red "End Call" button on his cell phone in the middle of Evelyn's sentence. "Did you hear what she said?"

"I'm already feeling nauseous," said Michael, the most

sensitive of them all. "Do you think what she is saying could possibly be true?"

"All right," said Steve, "let's not panic. I suggest we call the guides who can't be very far behind us and have everyone walk up to the Redmond house. I feel certain this is some kind of weird joke. You know those sisters are nuts! Remember the city council meeting?"

Peter called Robert Corwin, the head guide, and told him to tell everyone to turn around and that they would be walking up to the Redmond house at the top of the island.

The hunters were angry and impatient to know why they were not continuing the hunt.

"What's going on?" several cried out in unison.

"Do you know how many hours I traveled to get here?" asked an Arab sheikh.

"Where are the deer? That's what I want to know!" demanded a prince.

"We want to hunt!"

Robert Corwin caught up with a fellow guide and said under his breath, "Hell, we knew there were no deer yesterday. I wonder what's really going on."

The hunting entourage arrived at the Redmond house an hour after Evelyn's phone call. The sisters were outside on the large front veranda, dressed in their deer costumes. To their left, high above them, was a large movie screen with a silent black-and-white film titled *The Deer of Deer Island*, produced and filmed by their grandfather some forty years earlier.

The movie showed grainy scenes of deer grazing quietly in the woods, mother deer walking with baby deer, and mature males with well-developed antlers.

The hunters and guides and Steve, Michael, Peter, and George were all silent. They seemed to be in a collective state of shock. There was a low murmur of voices speaking foreign languages in an undercurrent of sound. Suddenly, Prince Al Waleed Abdul-Aziz Abdullah shouted out in heavily accented

English,

"What is wrong? In my country, when there is an important event it is not allowed to stop like this. There would be serious punishment, a whipping, prison..."

He was interrupted in the middle of his sentence when Florence, through a microphone that caused her voice to boom and echo in the quiet morning, said,

"Welcome everyone, welcome to Deer Villa."

As she spoke, her three sisters danced and turned behind her in their deer costumes.

"On the screen is a film made in 1920 by our grandfather, Dr. Jason Redmond. He wanted to document the life and habits of our native deer that have lived a protected life on our island for many years."

Evelyn came forward, took the microphone from Florence, and continued, "Until recently, when the Wild Deer Rescue Association relocated the deer to..."

The Sheikh of Abu Dhabi interrupted shouting in Arabic, "هل تقول كنت قد اتخذت الغزلان بعيداً عن الجزيرة؟" ("Are you saying you have taken the deer away from the island?")

There was a moment of utter silence as everyone stared first at the Sheikh and then at the sisters. Suddenly there was the hum of everyone starting to speak.

"Are you telling us this is a scam?" shouted the guide from Beijing as the sisters formed a bizarre chorus line, kicking and dancing and singing in unison into the microphone:

"*Yes, that is what we are saying, there are no deer, no deer, no deer, we've saved the deer, the deer, the deer, the beautiful deer of Deer Island.*"

Steve, Michael, Peter, and George took off running down the hill, hunting caps, gloves, jackets, and bags falling willy-nilly as they ran in front of the angry group of hunters and guides. The sisters' voices echoed down the hill after them all.

EPILOGUE

No one has heard from the four men who comprised Team Deer and their wives since this event. And all has been quiet on the island except for the dozens of unanswered lawsuits and ongoing litigation.

Within a few days, the WDRA truck could be seen, this time in daylight, delivering the tagged deer that had been removed as part of the agreement made with the Redmond sisters.

With the reappearance of the deer, property values fell as many of the new residents listed their homes for sale, and eventually the quiet life of Deer Island returned.

ROSE THE ROSE: A BOTANICAL TALE

It's hard being a flower because your life is very short, especially if you are a rose. To begin with, my parents were part of a bush, and not a very kind or friendly bush, since its branches were armed with thorns, which I guess is okay, because I felt very protected. Actually, the branches are sweet on the inside, and every year they give birth dozens of times to little baby buds. The buds grow and get bigger and bigger until the soft green covering that was all over them begins to roll back and you can see the tiny beautiful baby inside. Anyway, enough about my creation.

I was born two days ago and I just opened my eyes! Whew...I can see something that looks very far away and very blue (when I was older I learned it was the sky). I am so small and I feel so safe and happy and sleepy. When I wake up I'm taller and feel a little bigger. There are lots of other little boys and girls and I just heard a human say,

"Look at all the buds."

I don't know how I know, but I have a strong feeling that I'm not just an ordinary rose bud...I'm special, and I know I'm going to be very pretty...maybe even beautiful.

Eeeeeuuuuu! I'm being sprayed all over. Ooooooh, what an awful feeling, but I hear the gardeners saying that I need vitamins, and actually, I'm beginning to feel healthier and stronger. Every day, I can't wait for the dawn and then the lightening sky and then the full sun. It all makes me a little stronger and a little bigger, which makes me happy. I look around and see that I have many sisters and brothers and I can hear humans and they are giving us names: Adelaide, Bella Diana, Danny Boy, Jacquelyn. Then when they get to me, silence. I can hear them breathing and then someone says,

"Oh my God, she is so beautiful!"

I can feel a gentle touch on my outermost petal.

"We can only give her one name since she is the essence of rose beauty. Her name is Rose...the Rose, a princess of all roses."

"No," another human says, "not a princess, she's a queen."

And so my life is off to an elegant start. All the other roses look up to me, and indeed I am pretty and tall and as I open my petals I can hear all the oohs and ahs...and then all of a sudden, I am grown up. I feel my pale lavender petals so soft and velvety moving ever so slightly with the breeze. I feel true happiness for a few hours and then I begin to feel thirsty, very thirsty, and hear some humans saying that we are in a drought, and that the well that gives us our water is dry.

I can hear my brothers and sisters crying and moaning and then actually singing while dancing for rain. And then I hear scary deep voices. I look up and it is the trees chanting,

"Rain, rain, come, rain, you must come, rain..."

I am feeling weaker and weaker and I can no longer hold on to my petals; they begin to fall, one by one. I must have fallen asleep; then something really hard hits me right on my most beautiful surviving petal face. It wakes me up and I feel lots of drops. Yes, it is raining!

I feel my petals drinking and drinking and growing stronger. Then, very faintly, I can hear my brothers and sisters in their lovely soprano voices singing *Raindrops keep falling on my head*...and then in deep baritone voices the trees sing, *Raindrops on roses and whiskers on kittens*...and I feel so happy and a little sleepy. Another song soon escapes my own lips:

Good night ladies, good night ladies, good night ladies, I have to leave you now...

A LOVE AFFAIR

Mary's husband passed away when she was sixty-six years old. They had been married for thirty years without any real intimacy.

She resigned herself to living the remainder of her life independent and alone. Although her thirty-year marriage had been devoid of true intimacy and companionship, she had four children and nine grandchildren who all loved her and she them. Mary's son, John, once wrote to his siblings on Mother's Day:

Mom is bigoted, opinionated, and sometimes downright daffy in her approach to life. She is fearful of cats, intruders, airplanes, eucalyptus trees, and official-looking documents yet she'll boldly challenge any gambling establishment, be it a casino or racetrack. She will aggressively operate an automobile to the point of recklessness; her commitment toward her work as a hospital volunteer borders on fanaticism and her lifelong war against dust, dirt, and cobwebs is legendary. She is also compassionate, giving, understanding and supportive, and I love her, she's our Mom.

Mary prided herself on being a lady and she worked very hard to keep up this pretense by way of her social standing in the community, her immaculate appearance, and by surrounding herself with material things. She went to the beauty parlor once a week, and, between appointments, wrapped her head in toilet paper to keep her heavily sprayed hair in place. She also had a weekly manicure, and a pedicure once a month. She employed a laundry pick-up and delivery service as she never ironed but loved the family's clothes, kitchen towels, and bed linens to be washed, starched and pressed. Mary said supermarkets made her dizzy so, while leaning out the window with cigarette in hand, she'd order her groceries over the phone to either Mario or June, a couple who owned the small grocery and butcher store nearby.

Her house was spotlessly clean and remained appointed exactly the same as when the interior decorator had arranged it back in 1952 when she and her second husband bought the lovely ranch-style home, which had been photographed and appeared in one of the issues of *House Beautiful*.

During this thirty-year marriage, Mary filled her days by volunteering as a Pink Lady at Marin General Hospital several times a week, participating as a member of a local fundraising social group, meeting monthly with her bridge club, and lunching at the St. Francis Yacht Club whenever her oldest son invited her.

During the first year of her widowhood, she became friendly with Sue, who was also a volunteer at the hospital. They started socializing together and dined at their favorite restaurants: Fleur de Lys, Maurice et Charles, The Velvet Turtle, and Sabella's, to name a few. They also enjoyed shopping, but what they loved most were their frequent gambling trips to Reno and Lake Tahoe.

Mary loved to gamble. She discovered this on her first trip to Reno where, at age thirty-three, she'd lived for six weeks while getting divorced from her first husband. Reno claims to be the "Biggest Little City in the World" and Mary couldn't have agreed more with that declaration. It was her haven, her escape, her excitement. Her introduction to gambling was by playing the nickel slot machines, and, emboldened by success, she learned to play Black-Jack and Craps.

On a balmy May evening in 1976, Sue called and said, "Would you like to go with me to dinner at San Rafael Joe's?" Mary thought that would be a nice idea. They met at the bar of the restaurant while waiting for their table. Mary ordered her usual, a dry Manhattan, up with a twist. There was a man sitting on her right and, although she noticed him, he was looking straight ahead in what appeared to be a fog. After some time had elapsed, she looked over at him and said,

"Excuse me, would you mind pretending to be my

boyfriend? The man standing behind my girlfriend and me is annoying and won't stop talking to me."

"Pardon me, m'am ?" he said.

"I said, would you please pretend you are my boyfriend?"

"Huh?"

"Oh, never mind, just look at me and I'll do the rest," she said.

"Ah, well, ma'am, I don't . . ."

Whereupon she put her hand on his right shoulder and animatedly threw her head back toward the ceiling while laughing out loud at nothing.

"Ah, ma'am , well, I've never been a boyfriend before," he said.

"Really? You ought to try it some time. It can be lots of fun. What's your name? Mine's Mary."

"I'm called Bill."

"What brings you to San Rafael Joe's, Bill?" she asked.

"Well, ma'am . . ."

"Call me Mary."

"Yes, ma'am, well, I've been wantin' to see the Giants play for many a year now and I decided I could take a couple of days off my farm and come down here. I saw them today and they won. It was pretty darn exciting. I looked on the map and found this here town of San Rafe-e-el and found this little motel down the street and thought it would be better stayin' here than trying to find a place in San Francisco. I'm not too keen on big cities. You see, I've lived in Oregon all my life. I grow trees and raise a few head of sheep."

"My, that sounds interesting. Oregon, what part?" Mary liked him for some reason, his naiveté maybe. He looked and smelled clean, maybe that was it.

"A little town called Coos Bay. Most people haven't heard of it. Have you?"

"No, I've never been to Oregon. I was actually born in San Francisco and have never been out of California."

Just then Sue came up and Mary introduced them. Sue asked if he wanted to join them for dinner and to everyone's surprise Bill said he would.

During dinner the conversation turned to Reno as Mary and Sue were leaving the next day for a weekend of gambling. They had had enough to drink so they were both a bit friendlier than usual. "Have you ever been to Reno?" Mary asked.

"Nope, can't say's I have. Until tonight, I've never even stayed in a motel."

"Well, do you want to come with us? We always stay at Harrah's and the rooms are beautifully appointed. We order room service and have breakfast in bed."

"Oh, ma'am, I never ate breakfast in bed before!" And then he laughed for a long time on that one.

"Call me Mary, please. Do you like to gamble?" she asked.

"Don't know, I've never gambled before."

"I'll show you how; it's easy and it's lots of fun and who knows, you might win some money at the same time," Mary said.

"Well, I'd like that, ma'am ...I mean, Mary."

The next day, they caravanned to Reno and decided they could share a room as there were two double beds. Bill seemed to be in shock; he could neither agree nor disagree with all their decisions as things were going far too fast for him.

As soon as they arrived, Sue hooked up with her occasional boyfriend, leaving Mary and Bill to their own devices.

Mary seized the opportunity to share her enthusiasm for gambling and immediately introduced Bill to her passion.

"First, we'll go to the slots," she explained. "That's an easy way to learn how to play Black-Jack without having to be intimidated by others being around. We might as well go to the quarter Black-Jack slots, there's no point in wasting our time with anything less. I suggest you put in the maximum of five coins because if you hit the jackpot, a royal flush, it will not pay much if you put in only one or two quarters and then you'd kick yourself as I did once," she said, always the optimist.

He reluctantly sat down and Mary tutored him while he cranked the handle. Pretty soon they were both laughing and marveling at how the tray filled with clanking quarters. The background din of bells and whistles increased both their heart rates. She had a convert, right then and there. He won back his money and then some and so it went. This positive experience whet his appetite for more and Mary loved seeing him having such a good time.

"Are you ready for the real thing?" she asked. "Let's take $20 and go sit at a real Black-Jack table. Look, that table's almost empty so it's a good time to go. One thing though, don't sit at the first or last seats — those are called first base and third base. You'll want to know the ropes and rules before you sit in either of those or else you'll get the other players mad. Now remember, if the dealer is showing a face card or a 10, and your cards total 12, assume her other card, the one facing down, is a 10. Are you following me?" She could see his eyes were glazing over.

"No, stop, I can't remember all that."

She realized the nuances of the game were going to come to him slowly and decided to forget about giving out more information. She said,

"Never mind. The dealers are usually very friendly and helpful. We'll go slowly. Just follow me."

And with that Mary was gone like a shot. You never could keep up with her when she was heading for a gambling table.

He followed the basic rules and they played with their original $20 for over two hours and, as Mary suggested,

"Once in a while you'll have a feeling and you'll want to hit a card that you probably shouldn't, but do it anyway. That's why it's called gambling. You may just get lucky."

By the end of the weekend, Bill had learned to play Black-Jack, Keno, Roulette, and a smidge of Craps. He had a wonderful time and just kept scratching his head at all the glitter and glitz of Reno and he couldn't believe how many noisy, crowded, and exciting casinos and scantily dressed cocktail waitresses this little city had.

By the end of the weekend, they pooled their earnings and were thrilled to find that all expenses were essentially negated by their winnings.

Just before they departed, Mary gave Bill her phone number and they both returned to their hometown routines. About a month later, while Mary was cooking dinner for her granddaughter, the phone rang.

"Hi, Mary, this here's Bill, I thought I'd come down to San Rafe-e-el again and go see a Giants game, what are you doin'?"

Mary was surprised how her heart raced when she heard his voice. She didn't expect to feel so excited. She immediately invited him to come to her house and stay while he was in town. Again, they had a great time and it surprised them both how easy it was to be with one another.

During this visit, Mary asked Bill if he had ever been to a horse race. His reply, as usual, was "Nope, can't say's I have."

And with that, her eagerness to teach him about her second passion, horse racing, came alive. He again was an enthusiastic student as she talked about Golden Gate Fields, Bay Meadows, and all the other California tracks that had horse races throughout the year. They picked up a Daily Racing Form from the 881 Club in San Rafael and she taught him how to pick a horse, decipher the codes on the program, and shared with him what she knew about the various jockeys, trainers, and owners.

She told him which horses were good on grass and which ran better in mud and rain, which horses had won and which were upstarts. They plowed through forms, tips, and programs and then went to Golden Gate Fields for Bill's first horse race.

Mary led Bill down to where the horses came out so they could look them over and watch the jockeys weigh in. The smell of the horses, turf, saddles, and sweat excited Mary's senses and again she told him,

"You can know all about the odds and who the tippers claim are the winning horses, but if you have a feeling about one, pick it. That's why it's called gambling."

She often picked horses by just a feeling and, if a horse had one of her children's names in it, she'd always choose that horse to win, or, if the horse was gray , she'd usually pick that one as so often a gray horse won. Although Mary's bets were always limited to $2.00 across the board, she might as well have bet $2,000, so great was her thrill as the horses bolted from the gate and the nervous anticipation she felt in hoping that maybe her 'favorite' would be the first to cross the finish line.

Mary's luck at the track was equal to her luck at the tables and although her winnings were never big, they usually paid for the day's outing. Bill was lucky, too, and he couldn't believe how often he'd go to the teller to collect for a winning bet.

Bill stayed for a whole month that first visit and he and Mary went to the race track almost daily. But as unexpectedly as Bill's arrival had been, his announcement in the middle of a clear starry night that he was leaving and his subsequent departure were so rapid, it was as if his being there at all had been a mirage.

Weeks passed and they wrote occasionally to one another. Their notes were very superficial and never touched on any feelings or emotions and Bill never indicated that a trip to San Rafael might be forthcoming.

Then one day Mary got another unexpected phone call with that now familiar voice saying,

"Hi Mare, I'm on my way down. I'll see you in a day or two."

This began a pattern. Bill would call and Mary's whole life turned upside down. She'd take a leave from volunteering, be unavailable for any family outings or social events, and primp and plan in great anticipation of Bill's arrival. He'd walk in the door with a big smile on his face and from then on the two of them were like children giggling and laughing at what appeared to those around them to be nothing. Eventually, Bill's visits became more frequent and longer so that he was more often in California than in Oregon.

Mary's family and friends couldn't understand what she

possibly could see in Bill because he and Mary were nothing alike. Not only was there a fifteen year difference in their ages (he being the younger), he was what one might call a country bumpkin. He wore nothing but blue jeans and a snap shirt with a t-shirt underneath, work boots, and a wide leather belt. He was extremely self-conscious and awkward at any gathering or social event, and he literally bumbled his way through every get-together, saying inane things, thinking he was 'hip,' or laughing constantly at nothing and looking at his boots.

He had a peculiar way of sliding his tongue all the way out of his mouth just before he would respond to a question and, unfortunately, everyone imitated him when he wasn't looking. It got so bad that all her children, before responding to each other, started with the tongue projection, and anyone who caught a glimpse of these antics must have thought the whole family was nuts.

Mary, on the other hand, ever so chic, was always tastefully and appropriately dressed, dripping in jewels, wearing her favorite perfume, White Shoulders. She knew all the proper social graces but when it came to Bill all would melt away and she would stand next to him looking up into his eyes as he'd ramble on about something off the wall, and you could just see her swoon. He loved attention, being a Leo, and she gave it to him.

Though her family and friends wondered aloud about this strange relationship, you couldn't help but like them as a couple. They had such fun together and were always laughing. It really was joyful to see.

Time passed and months turned into years and almost two decades later they were still rendezvousing in the same way: out of the blue he would appear, stay for an extended period, and then in the middle of the night depart. Their outings expanded into sightseeing trips to Yellowstone National Park, Yosemite National Park, Bryce Canyon, Crater Lake, Shasta Lake, Carmel, Monterey, and all the state fairs in California where horse racing took place in the summers. Bill and Mary saw so many sites that she would never have seen were it not for Bill and she cherished their time together.

Bill, however, remained mysterious in his dual life and throughout the years he continued to spontaneously leave, which was heartbreaking to Mary, who quietly accepted it. She would just shrug her shoulders, sigh, and say, "What can I do?"

On her 86th birthday, Mary was diagnosed with lung cancer. Bill happened to be visiting at the time. This news was not discussed between them, although he knew of her diagnosis. That night he quietly took his things and left.

Many months went by, the longest span of time that they hadn't been together, and Mary knew he wasn't coming back. When asked why she wasn't angry or hurt or sad, she responded,

"What good would that do? There's no point in dwelling on it." And that was that.

It was a year and a half before she became bedridden and her family remained steadfast in her care while she silently and stoically dwindled into a frail, ill, old lady.

When hospice came in, her family knew the end was near and all gathered around. They were holding her hand and stroking her brow when all of a sudden she opened her eyes and lifted her head slightly and stared into the corner across the room.

"Who's that?" she asked. "That man, over there? Bill, Bill is that you?" Then she put her head down and with a smile on her face she peacefully drifted away.

A SURPRISE ENDING

Part One

In the medical building elevator, as she and Michael were coming down from a visit with his doctor, Evelyn had an epiphany; now she knew what to do and how she was going to do it. Doctor Vincent had confirmed that her husband had high cholesterol and a heart condition. Evelyn was sixty-six years old and even though her husband was nine years younger, he was not as healthy as she. He was not careful about his diet, loved steak and French fries, smoked cigars, and rarely exercised.

In contrast, Evelyn, who had been Michael's secretary before she married him, was careful about her diet, had a personal strength trainer, practiced yoga, walked each day with her women friends, and slept well each night.

Her longtime lover, Robert, had recently given her an ultimatum: get a divorce and come live with him, or break off their relationship. Her dilemma was that she enjoyed the way she lived; her husband Michael was a rich man, while Robert was living on an Army veteran's pension, not allowing for the lifestyle to which she'd become accustomed.

Evelyn and Michael lived in Michael's family house on the Battery with views of Charleston Harbor. She had full-time household help, a car and driver, designer clothing, and expensive jewelry. She had signed away Michael's family money in their pre-nuptial agreement in case of divorce. If she divorced him she would get nothing, but if he were to die from natural causes, she would inherit his fortune. She did not want to divorce, as she did not want to "fall from grace," which was how she had come to think of it.

Having just been counseled by Michael's doctor about the importance of diet for a person with high cholesterol and a heart condition, she began making a plan. Evelyn and her girlfriends had often traveled abroad on cooking tours of The Great Chefs, sitting in the kitchens of famous European restaurants while the chefs demonstrated "the art of fine cooking..." Consequently, she knew a lot about food, including the secret to great French cuisine, which could, and had been summed up as:

"*Butter, butter, give me more butter.*"

Now, after this visit with Michael's doctor and the importance that was placed on eliminating fat from his diet, she knew she had to change everything. No more butter and no more cream; chicken breasts with no skin and veggie burgers instead of Mike's favorite double burgers with extra mayo and cheese.

But another sort of diet plan began to form in Evelyn's mind...maybe now she could have everything. If Michael were to die of natural causes she would be the sole recipient of his sizable estate. Having developed her cooking skills, she told Michael he needn't worry since she could still make his food taste wonderful even though she would be careful to eliminate the fats.

Part Two

Michael smiled upon hearing Evelyn's plan. Later, he took her hand and said, "Darling, you are so sweet, I have a surprise for you. I have hired the well-known French Chef, Alain Moreau (at great expense, I want you to know!), who understands my health problems, and has signed an agreement for one year, to cook and deliver delicious, rich-tasting meals, that are actually low-fat, or what he calls 'light cooking.' And so, my dear wife, you will not have to bother with cooking for the entire year..."

Evelyn smiled in response and said,

"Michael, you are wonderful!"

She felt the cell phone she kept exclusively for Robert vibrating in her handbag. She read the text: *Evelyn, I've decided not to see you anymore as long as you are married to Michael. If you decide to leave him, you know I will always be here for you.*

She immediately felt a deep loss and knew that now she

would have to come up with another plan quickly. Michael was an insomniac and a long-time user of Tamazepam, a strong medication to induce sleep. One Tamazepam was all he needed for a full night's rest. What if he were to have more?

"Darling," she said to Michael, "you know our twenty-fifth anniversary is coming up next month. Let's go on a romantic cruise. We can invite Alain to join us so he can maintain your special diet."

Michael agreed, and Evelyn began making arrangements on the Blue Air's Blue Cloud cruise ship, which cost nearly $100,000 for the three of them.

Part Three

Evelyn booked the Regent Suite on the ship for the three of them. She was excited and told Michael the details over dinner that evening.

"First of all," she began, "our calendar is cleared for three weeks in June; and I booked the Regent Suite, which is approximately the same size as our house. It has three bedrooms and baths, a private garden, a chef's kitchen for Alain, and 24-hour butler and maid service."

Michael said, "Let me give you a kiss darling – you do everything so elegantly. I'll tell Alain in the morning."

The next day, he asked Alain if he would like to join them.

"What do you think?" Alain responded. "Yes, I would very much like to join you. Twenty years ago, I was a chef on an ocean liner and I'll never forget the experience."

Packing for the ship, Evelyn very carefully made sure that all of Michael's medications were in place, particularly an ample supply of his Tamazepam. Feeling lonely and unwanted by no longer having her lover Robert and by her husband Michael's inability to have sex, she began looking at Alain with different eyes. She realized that he was quite attractive, and even better, at least twenty years younger than she was.

Their departure date arrived and their driver dropped them at the entrance of the Charleston Cruise Port, where they were greeted by their personal butler, Lane, and escorted onto the ship and into their luxurious accommodations. They stood on their private balcony as the ship slowly backed away from the dock and out into the open sea. That evening, Alain made an incredible dinner of Escargots, followed by Coq au Vin, and accompanied by a lovely bottle of Bordeaux.

After they retired to their rooms, Evelyn took a long, luxurious bath, put on a sheer silk nightgown, and walked out of her room into Alain's room. Evelyn slipped into bed next to him where they made passionate love.

Afterward, Evelyn returned to her room, where Michael found her in the morning.

"Sleep well?" he asked. "Very well," she responded.

And so the days passed with lovely walks, elegant food and wines, music, and nightly entertainment in the main Salon of the ship.

One night after they had made love, Evelyn told Alain how much she would miss him if they were to part, and that if she were to divorce Michael, according to the prenups she had signed, she would receive no part of his fortune.

"However," she said, "if he dies naturally, we can be together and live like we do now. I don't know if you know that Michael is on Tamazepam for his sleep disorder. If you were to put an overdose into his food or wine..."

The next night Alain served Michael his favorite dish, Coquilles Saint-Jacques, laced with large amounts of Tamazepam. Michael fell asleep at the table, and they both carried him into his room, put him in his pajamas, and into his bed.

In the morning, Evelyn told the butler that she could not wake Michael and that he should call the doctor. The ship's doctor pronounced him dead. Evelyn was told that she could request an autopsy upon their return, and the three of them were airlifted by helicopter from the ship back home. After the autopsy, Michael's death was found to be an overdose of sleeping pills, and Evelyn the recipient of the estate.

As the months passed, Evelyn began to fear that Alain was losing interest in her and she suggested that they marry. After much discussion over the large estate, Alain agreed to sign a prenup stating that in the event of a divorce, he would not be a recipient of her estate. However, in the event of her natural death, the entire estate would go to him, which in fact it did, when only a year after their marriage, Evelyn died after falling down the grand staircase of their elegant home.

And Alain lived quite happily ever after.

PLASTIC JESUS, PART 3

One incredibly bright, beautiful morning, I am dozing, warmed and relaxed by the sun, when I see Bobby's face next to mine through the windshield, though he is a bit hard to recognize. His light-colored hair is long and pulled straight back into a ponytail. The skin under his large, pale blue eyes is darker than the rest of his face and he has a sparse, scraggly beard. His broad shoulders are hunched forward and his flowered, short-sleeved shirt hangs over his faded jeans. I feel happy to see him as it immediately makes me think of Violet.

"I'll take this one," he says to the beaming Marvelous Marvins salesman standing nearby. They disappear for awhile, then Bobby returns alone and gets into the truck.

"I bought this truck because of you," he says, turning me around so that I face him and the inside of the truck. "My old Auntie Violet, who saved my life, had a statue just like you on the dashboard of her car." He smiles a little and then says, nodding,

"My name's Bobby, and I'm pleased to meet you!"

His hands are damp and cold against my body. As I peer into his face I feel a little frightened remembering how tightly he held me the last time, and also that he wanted Auntie Violet dead.

We drive around the rest of the day and into the night, and every day after that. At night he parks the truck in Violet's garage, a place I am familiar with. Unlike when I was with Violet, we go out for drives every day. We drive all over the city, out to Pinewood and then back to the city. And, like his Auntie Violet, Bobby carries on a continuous monologue, always directed at me. Sometimes he seems to wait for an answer or a sign that I am listening. Often I get that tingling and a feeling that I want to respond but it goes away before I can really do anything about it.

Meanwhile, I am having so many exciting experiences; I'm overwhelmed by all I see of the world and can't think of anything else. I love looking at the blue sky and seeing white puffy clouds float by and having to close my eyes when we drive into the sun.

One day, in the truck, Bobby surprises me with a new revelation.

"Sweet Jesus," he confides, "Auntie Violet found me stuffed inside a garbage can right after I was born. My mother didn't want me. I will never know who my father was. I always felt different from the other kids, embarrassed that my Aunt looked so much older than the other parents at school. I was scared to leave school because the other boys would push me and make me fight with them. I used to hide under the bleachers after school and cry."

As he continues to talk about his feelings being hurt and how unhappy he was, I get that tingling feeling again, but even more than before. I want to say something. But what? And how?

One morning, we're driving as usual; it is very early in the morning, just beginning to get light. I think I see him first, a man coming toward us along the opposite side of the street next to a long line of parked cars. He's staggering, holding onto the cars, falling down, getting up and then falling again. When Bobby sees him, he slows way down and stops. My back is to him but I hear him say, "Hey Jesus, let's have a little fun!"

Suddenly he speeds up and it looks as if he's going to run into the man, but at the last second he screeches to a stop, then he backs up, and does it again, two or three more times, stopping each time just before hitting him. I see the terrified expression on the drunken man's face and hear him yell,

"HELP! HELP! HELP!"

Once again the tingling starts in my body, and I feel my face getting hot; I want to help but I cannot move.

After a while, I calm down and am enjoying the warmth of the sun when I feel Bobby's cold hands turn me around, and he confesses,

"I used to write stories about my dreams of torturing dogs and cats, and my ideas of kidnapping children; then Auntie discovered my journal, and committed me to Pinewood. I was so sad and so lonely."

I feel the pain I see on his face and an enormous shiver goes through my plastic body as I fall to the floor. Bobby picks me up and looks into my face before he replaces me on my stand.

Shortly after that, he tells me his plan, long in the making.

"Hey, Jesus," he begins, excitement in his voice. "One day soon, I'm going to kidnap a kid!"

I want to ask him why, but I can't, and then he tells me anyway.

"It'll force people to notice me, to pay attention to me."

I have to admit that as much as I love driving around and being able to see the world with Bobby, I have a scared feeling when he talks about kidnapping. I try not to listen and to concentrate more on everything I see out in the world every day. Like the birds flying high in the sky. I love how they come down to rest for a moment on the back of a bench or the edge of a fence, settle down, turn their heads this way and that, be quiet, then suddenly lift their wings and fly off into the sky.

One day, we park alongside a playground. Through the truck window, I can see a little boy on the swings. He is about six years old, with light brown hair, blue eyes, and rosy cheeks. We sit and watch him for a long time.

The next day Bobby parks there again, gets out of the truck, and approaches the boy. Within a short time they return to the truck together. We drive to a toy shop and they disappear inside. I watch the child's happy face as he comes out of the shop holding a large, colorful plastic bag.

As we drive, Bobby completely ignores me now, intent upon his conversation with the boy. He asks him all kinds of questions in a new softer voice that I haven't heard before.

"You know, my name is Bobby, too!" he says to the little boy. "So I'm going to call you Little Bobby, and I'll be Big Bobby. What do you think of that?"

"I guess it's okay," the boy replies.

"What do you eat for breakfast?" Big Bobby asks, and then, "Do you eat dinner with your mother and father or just with your mother?" and "Do you have a lot of friends in school?" and, "Are the other kids nice to you?"

The boy answers mostly with a "yes" or a "no" and then says, "When can I play with my toys?"

"Right now," Bobby answers. We park in front of a picnic area.

They get out of the truck, taking a picnic basket, a blanket, and the bag of toys with them. They lay the blanket under a massive oak tree, and I watch as they eat lunch and play together with the new toys, little trucks and cars, and lots of small colored plastic figures of people that they can bend and place in the little cars and trucks.

I know something is wrong when I see the boy stand up, shake his head no, then start to run away. Bobby runs after him, grabs his arm and pulls him to the truck. He opens the door and pushes him into the passenger seat.

"I wanna go home now," says the boy, starting to cry.

Bobby sits in the driver's seat; he turns me around, and stares at me for a long time. I see his shoulders hunch and hear him start to sob.

As I watch, I feel the tingling again, stronger, a vibration from my insides out. But this time it's much stronger than ever before, taking over my entire body. I really feel Bobby's pain and I want to comfort him. As Little Bobby and I watch, I hear his child's voice and feel his small hands take me off my stand.

"You're just like the statue in our church," he says staring at me. "You're supposed to help people. Please help me now!" he pleads, holding me for a little while before putting me carefully back on my stand.

Before long, Big Bobby's sobbing stops and he pulls a white handkerchief from his pocket, blows his nose and wipes his eyes. Then I feel his hand, usually cold but now warm, around my body as he brings me so close to his face that I can feel his breath.

"Help me, help me, help me..." he repeats over and over. He is holding me so tightly that I am having trouble catching my breath, when suddenly I realize that I am breathing, taking huge gulps of air, something I have never done before. I breathe so long and so deep I feel that I am going to burst.

Then, deep inside me, starting at my feet, a stinging, prickly feeling grows stronger and stronger. I close my eyes and feel myself shake. I fall out of Big Bobby's hand, onto the seat next to Little Bobby, and then onto the floor. There is a flash of light, and I hear a loud crash as I explode.

When the blackness ends I am awake and sitting behind the wheel of my truck. I touch my face and see my hands on the steering wheel. They are mine and yet they are not. I have become Bobby. Next to me in the passenger seat is the boy, his eyes closed. On the floor, at the boy's feet, are broken pieces of cream-colored plastic.

As I look at the sleeping boy, a feeling of regret washes over me. "Oh my God, what have I done?"

I hold Little Bobby's hand and concentrate hard on his waking up.

"Please take me home," he whispers.

"Yes, of course."

I drive back to the playground, overwhelmed by a feeling of compassion and remorse. I want to make Little Bobby feel better, and I want him to not be scared any more. At the playground he asks, "Can I take my toys?"

"Yes."

"All of them?" he asks, looking up at me.

"Yes, you can take them with you; they are yours to play with whenever you want."

I watch as he runs down the street to the corner, crosses at the green light, and walks up to the brick house. He waits at the door and soon disappears inside.

THE END

THE DOWRY

Part I

Jane pushed open the carved wooden doors of the coffee house and entered the small, smoky room. She looked around for Susan, but didn't see her even though she herself was a little late. Jane was shy and didn't want to walk across the room and sit down alone. She'd decided to go outside to wait when a waiter approached.

"Do you want a table, *señorita?*"

"Yes. I mean, *si, por favor.*"

He led her to a small table in the corner of the room. She sat down, immediately feeling a little more secure.

"Only for one?" he asked, handing her a menu.

"No, uh, *una otra persona,*" she said, turning to look at the doors.

"*Si, señorita,*" he nodded, and left another menu on the table.

Jane pretended to read the menu, looking around the room once again. She was twenty-two and this was her first time out of the United States, her second day in Mexico City, her first real separation from her parents.

She glanced over at four young Mexican men seated several tables away. They had turned their chairs so they were facing her, and were all staring and smiling boldly. She felt the blood rush to her face and looked away, embarrassed.

Jane looked down at the menu again; where was Susan?

It was early May. She had her teaching credential, and in September was going to start her first job as a kindergarten teacher in San Diego, her hometown. Her childhood friend, Susan Valenti, was studying anthropology at the University of Mexico in Mexico City, and had invited Jane to stay with her and the family she was living with for the summer. Since Jane's new job was to be in a Spanish-speaking school district, this seemed like the ideal place for her to visit. Determined to improve her Spanish, she had enrolled in the University of the Americas.

Now, she reached into her large travel bag, pulled out her Spanish phrase book, and tried to read the Spanish words, saying them to herself as she read. Why were they watching her like that? Were they flirting with her? What if they approached her?

The waiter's voice broke into her thoughts. He had returned, pad in hand, and was saying something indistinguishable to her.

"Please repeat," she managed to say.

He repeated himself, still incomprehensible to her.

"*Yo* no understand," she replied, feeling very uncomfortable.

One of the four young men approached her table.

"The waiter, he would like to know if you wish to order something. A drink, perhaps?"

He was standing next to her. She stared at him, at his olive complexion, his dark eyes, his long dark hair tied in a ponytail.

"Please tell him I would like to wait for my friend to arrive first," she said, managing a smile.

He conveyed the message to the waiter who nodded and walked away.

"What is your name?" the young man asked her in English with a strong Mexican accent.

"Jane Baker."

"Jane," he said, "your hair, your eyes, you are beautiful, you are the girl I want to marry."

The blood rushed to her face again.

"Please, Jane," he said, looking serious now, "what is your phone number so that I may call you. You need not be frightened; I come from a good family. I do not normally approach a strange woman in a public place, but when I saw you needed a little help, well, I think you are so beautiful, I had no choice."

She smiled at his flattery and his formal manner of speech.

She was reluctant to give him her Mexican cell, as she knew her parents would not approve. She was quiet for a moment and realized she was feeling rebellious for the first time in her twenty-two years. But here she was, on her own. Maybe it was time to do something a little dangerous. Jane looked up at him.

"My number is 114-6566," she heard herself say.

He took his cell phone from his coat pocket and quickly entered her name and number. He bowed slightly.

"*Muchas gracias, señorita.* I believe your friend is here," he said, looking toward the entrance at a tall, fair-skinned girl with long, straight, blonde hair.

"Oh, please forgive my oversight," he continued. "My name is Youssef Abboud. I shall call you tomorrow." He walked back to his table, said something to his companions, and left the restaurant.

Susan sat down, breathlessly.

"Who were you talking to?" she asked, and without waiting for an answer went on. "I'm so sorry about being late," she said. "I have to tell you what happened, you probably won't believe this, but...."

She talked on, but Jane wasn't listening. Instead, she thought about what Youssef had said. She knew she stood out in Mexico with her fair skin and blonde curly hair, but no one had ever told her they wanted to marry her. She was filled with excitement and felt slightly dizzy. She wanted to think about what had just happened to her. She contrasted him with David, her steady boyfriend in college. She smiled. In comparison, Youssef Abboud appeared so suave, so polished and continental, so sure of himself.

David had been the only serious male friendship in her life. They had gone together her last two years in college. Because of her shyness with men, she seldom was asked out on dates, and was relieved when David, equally shy and unassertive, had gently pursued her. She agreed to "go steady" because he was so kind to her. She had never fancied herself in love with him, and had never made love with him. She was a virgin. They would kiss good night, and the few times that David pressed her to go further, she simply told him that she couldn't, since she did not love him, and he understood. When school ended, their relationship did also, quietly, just as it had begun.

Her thoughts, however, had always been filled with fantasies of handsome men and passionate love affairs. She felt exhilarated and tremendously excited at the prospect of this actually happening to her. Now, finally, she was away from her parents and her hometown, on her own for the first time, and ready to start her own life.

"Jane, I asked you a question. You aren't listening," Susan said. "Who was that guy you were talking to?"

"I'm sorry, Sue. I'm so happy you're here. It's just that I was feeling really anxious waiting for you," she paused and continued, "and the guy I was talking to asked me for my phone number and I gave it to him!"

"Whoa, that doesn't sound like you!"

"I know, Sue. I'm changing. I think I'm finally ready for an adventure!"

Sue reached across the table and gently squeezed her friend's hand. "We've been friends for a long time," she said.

"Let's order some food. I'm hungry," said Jane.

Part II

Jane kept checking her cell for a call she might have missed. It was almost five o'clock the next day, and she was in the bedroom she shared with Sue. Youssef had not called. The happiness she had been feeling was being replaced with disappointment.

Jane was an only child, born late in her parents' lives. When she was small, they'd fretted over her constantly — no babysitters; Jane accompanied them everywhere. She was not allowed to walk to school by herself, only six blocks from where they lived, until she was in junior high.

Her mother was forever concerned with what Jane wore, how she was feeling, and what she wanted. She was the center of her parents' lives, and rarely did anything independent of them. She grew up vacillating between feeling happy in her dependence on her parents and wanting to break away from them. It was in one of her periods of wanting independence that her best friend Susan had invited her to join her in Mexico City for the summer. Now her telephone rang.

"Is this *Señorita* Jane," a voice asked softly, "*con los ojos bonitas*?"

"Youssef!"

He asked her for dinner that evening. Her mouth was dry as she told him that dinner would be lovely.

"Will you be ready at nine?" he asked.

"Yes. I will be waiting."

"Where do you live?" he asked.

She told him her address.

"*Si, si.* See you *mas tarde!*" he said.

She heard the click as he hung up, and drew a long breath to calm herself. She called her parents in San Diego to tell them she was fine, how much she loved them, and hoped they were not missing her too much. She went to her closet and decided on a new dress, one she had not worn before.

As she soaked in the tub, she thought about Youssef Abboud. Who was he? Definitely not a Mexican name. Sounded Middle Eastern. She loved that he told her that her eyes were beautiful. She wondered if he would kiss her or perhaps try to make love to her that evening. She was ready now. She shivered in anticipation.

Positive feelings washed over her, she was so glad she had come to Mexico, grateful to Susan for inviting her to visit. Susan came into the bathroom and sat on the edge of the tub.

"Hi, want to go out tonight after dinner?"

"Sorry, I have a date."

"A date? With who? You've only been here three days."

Jane put her head back on the bath pillow, and closed her eyes. "Sue, remember, last night I told you I met a guy and gave him my phone number."

"Right. So?"

"Okay, so, he called me today and invited me to dinner."

Susan looked at her friend and saw how happy she was.

"Jane," Susan said slowly, "that's great, but you need to know that Mexican men are different from the guys we know at home..."

"I'm twenty-two years old. Please don't act like my parents!"

Susan nodded, then stood. "You're right." On her way out of the bathroom, she stopped and smiled at Jane.

"You're way overdue for romance."

Part III

Youssef arrived at nine, and Jane introduced him to Susan. As she was leaving, she whispered in Susan's ear,

"Isn't he handsome?" Susan whispered back, "He's not Mexican, he looks Middle-Eastern."

Jane loved the feel of Youssef's strong hands as he helped her into his black Mercedes. She could not remember ever feeling happier.

He took her to a fancy French restaurant. Jane felt intimidated at first by the hovering waiters and the lavishness of the service. The white pillars around the room were trimmed in gold leaf. The gilded chairs had dark-red velvet seats. The tables had fine beige linen cloths and polished silverware. There was an orchestra of fourteen violins; she counted them.

"Youssef, will you order for me?" she asked after looking at the long menu in French.

"Of course, *Juana*. That's your name in Spanish, but I will call you Jane."

His black curly hair was shiny and perfectly styled. She

thought his dark skin and closely trimmed beard made him look like a movie star.

"You are so beautiful," he said. "I will talk only in English with you. I have studied it much on my own, including one summer of language camp in San Diego, California. Tell me, Jane, what are you doing here in Mexico City?"

Soon, the combination of champagne and Youssef's apparent familiarity and ease with the restaurant caused her to relax. The food tasted more delicious than any she had eaten before. They drank wine, and his hand, as he held hers across the table, felt comfortable and strong.

She was no longer self-conscious. She answered his many questions sweetly and willingly, delighted that he was interested in knowing about her, and she was not offended by his personal questions.

Where was she born? How old was she? Why did she come here? Did she ever have a boyfriend? What were her future plans? How many classes was she taking at the University of the Americas? Who were her teachers? She laughed when he asked her if she was rich.

"No," she replied, "I am not rich at all."

"If that is the case, how is it that you are able to travel and study at the University?"

By the end of the evening she had adjusted to his slightly superior, cool style. She tried to explain to him how middle-class Americans were able to send their children to a university. She told him that it was actually inexpensive for her to live here for the summer. She was unable to convince him of this, and his apparent naiveté about their two countries' comparative economics amused her.

"My beautiful Jane, I want to make love with you tonight," he said, as they were leaving the restaurant. "I live with my parents, and they would not approve of my bringing you home to my bed."

He took a room in a hotel so they could make love. He said

he wanted her and she felt the same about him. She did not feel frightened or strange; it all seemed very natural. Now she was no longer a virgin.

She saw him every day after that and lost interest in her classes. They visited museums, cathedrals, temples, and parks, and Youssef soon began talking of marriage. She acquired a taste for piquant Mexican food.

A month after their first date, Jane told Susan she was going to marry Youssef.

"Janie, that's insane. Please don't do anything so quickly! You're inexperienced in relationships with men."

"Sue, you know that I went with David for two years."

"You can hardly call that a serious relationship. This is different."

"What do you mean 'different?'"

"Youssef is Mexican with Middle-Eastern roots, Jane. His culture is totally different from ours."

"And what is that supposed to mean? That I shouldn't love anyone who is Mexican or Lebanese?"

"It means that his lifestyle is different from yours. It's difficult for an American to adjust to it, no matter how '*in love*' you think you are. Remember, this is my second year studying in Mexico."

Jane was angry at Susan's reaction and refused to discuss it further with her. They barely spoke to each other for the rest of the day.

That evening she told Youssef what had happened.

"*Mi amor*, is it not obvious to you that your friend is only jealous? It is very typical for a woman to feel that way when her friend is marrying before she is." He put his arms around her and held her. "I have told you often that it is an easy life for a woman in Mexico. You will be taken care of. You shall have no worries, no problems. You will only have to make me happy." She stayed in his arms, feeling his strength, feeling secure. "But now, my darling, we must find another house for you to live in.

We know other families with big houses."

Susan cried the afternoon she saw Youssef helping Jane with her suitcases. Jane wanted to talk things over with her as they had always done, but Youssef's strong hand was on her arm, urging her to come with him. So she did, looking back with sadness at her friend.

"I'll stay in touch, Sue, and you have my cell."

Youssef and Jane made love often, and afterward she would lie in his arms and they would talk. He told her how he had once aspired to become a doctor and had been accepted into medical school.

"Then, just at that time, my youngest sister Margarita had to have her first hip operation. It was a rare and unusual surgery and very expensive for my father. I am the oldest son. He needed my help in his business; I could not refuse him when he asked."

Youssef's voice dropped until it was almost inaudible to Jane. "So, you see, *mi carina*, here I am, twenty-seven years old, still working in my father's business. I am confessing to you, I do not like it. I have many good ideas for a business on my own, but I need uh ...*que es la palabra en Ingles*?" He hesitated a moment. "Capital! That is what you call it. I need capital in order to express my ideas. But now, it is late, we must sleep."

The next morning, when Jane awoke, Youssef was sitting on the edge of the bed. "*Mi vida*," he said suddenly, "how much dowry are your parents willing to give?"

"Dowry? What do you mean? What's a dowry?"

"Do you not know of our custom?" he replied. "It is customary in our family and many other Lebanese-Mexican families to receive money when a son marries, and to give money when a daughter marries."

Jane felt this was odd, not right, somehow. It was an old-fashioned idea she had read about in a history course. She moved away from him and sat up on the bed. "Well...I have nine thousand dollars in my savings account."

He burst into laughter, "Jane, you are so adorable. Nine

thousand dollars is a dowry for a poor Indian. That would never be acceptable to me or my family."

Cautiously, she asked, "How much would be acceptable then, Youssef?"

"I think ninety or one-hundred thousand would not be too much for you, an American."

She looked at him, her mouth suddenly dry. She felt unnerved and frightened. "But Youssef, my parents don't have that kind of money. And even if they did, I could never ask them for it. There must be another way. I would be happy to work while you go back to school or start your own business or whatever you want or..."

"No, I am sorry," he interrupted coldly. "You do not understand. Mexican women of our class do not work. If there is no dowry, there will be no marriage."

He sat up and got off the bed and began to dress.

"Jane, you are making me upset. I would like to take you to my home so you can see how a Mexican family like ours actually lives."

Part IV

He took her to meet his family, his mother, Mariam, and father, Emir, and six of his nine siblings. They received her coldly. Youssef had told her they did not approve of her because she was not Lebanese, not even Mexican.

They stood awkwardly in the entrance hall during the introductions. As she began to walk behind Youssef to the sofa, Emir stepped in front of her, reached out one hand, and buttoned the top button of her blouse. She was shocked but silent. Emir looked at her and said, "In our house, the women button their blouses."

She turned her eyes to Youssef whose look back was a serious warning to not say anything. Everyone sat down on large, ornate easy chairs and sofas in the big living room. The walls were covered with Muslim religious art. Every table surface was filled with painted antique jars and what she thought were vases, so different from what she knew. His mother picked up a little silver bell from the end table next to her and shook it.

Two young Mexican maids ran in and Mariam gave them instructions in rapid Spanish. They turned and left the room.

The family spoke no English to her, even though she knew they spoke at least conversational English. It tired and frustrated her to have to speak only Spanish, but she felt proud, when she saw Youssef admiring her, that she was able to at least get by in Spanish. The maids returned with plates of food, a mixture of tiny tacos and small Lebanese spinach pies. They ate sitting in the living room and when everyone was done, Jane got up to help collect the plates.

Youssef said,

"Jane, sit down, you are doing the maid's work."

They all looked at her as she sat down and Mariam rang the silver bell, and watched as the maids ran in and silently collected the plates. The maids brought coffee, and Youssef and his father and four brothers went into the library with their coffee to smoke cigars. She was left with the other women, Mariam and Youssef's two sisters. They talked in rapid Spanish about friends and shopping, and the daily visit to the hairdresser and the girls' prospects for marriage now that they were in their late teens.

When the men returned to the room, Youssef told her it was time to go. They said cool goodbyes and she was happy to leave. Youssef asked her how she liked his family, but did not respond when she told him they spoke so fast it was hard for her to understand them. He dropped her off without asking to come in. He said he was tired and he would see her tomorrow. She wondered if they had talked about the dowry.

Alone and quiet, she thought about the evening and how different Youssef's family was. She had learned that Youssef's sisters did not attend school beyond a year of high school for no other reason than it was not necessary; a woman stays in the home. They were seriously superstitious, arguing, for example, about who actually spoke first when the two sisters seemed to say the same word at the same time, because they believed that whoever was first would live the longest.

They were ostentatious, wearing too much jewelry and make-up; politically conservative, sincerely believing that women should not vote; and extremely religious, devoted Muslims because of their Lebanese roots.

She thought, *What have I done? I can't live this way, I need to get out of here.* But just thinking of not seeing Youssef was so painful that she resolved to find a way to like his family instead.

It was the end of August when Jane called her parents to introduce Youssef to them. Youssef got on the phone and formally asked Jane's father for her hand in marriage.

"And before you say anything," he said, "you must know that I am an honorable person, completely honest and a devoted and pious Muslim. I am part of my family's very successful refrigeration business and will always take care of your daughter in the best possible way."

Her parents were silent. "Jane, sweetheart," her mother finally said, "can we speak to you privately?"

Jane sighed, and asked Youssef to go into the other room.

"Okay, Mom, now what is it? Youssef's not here."

"Married? And to a Mexican-Muslim? Whom you have only known for three months? Not coming back to San Diego? Your return ticket is for next week! What about your new job, your career?"

The questions came swiftly. Jane wanted her parents to come to Mexico. They agreed to come the following week.

Part V

At the airport, Jane paced back and forth and took deep, rapid breaths as she waited for her parents. Looking down from the airport's upper level, she had a good view of everyone coming through customs. Her parents didn't see her, and as she watched them, she felt her deep love for them. Over the past few months she had been aware only of strong feelings toward Youssef. Now she felt torn between her parents and him.

They looked as if they had aged since she last saw them, only three months ago. Her father was sixty-seven, her mother sixty-four. They both were impeccably dressed and distinguished looking. She was proud of them. She loved her dad's gray , curly hair and horn-rimmed glasses. She watched her mother, still slender, hair tinted a tasteful light brown. She admired her poise and relaxed, direct manner, and wondered, as she often did, if she would be like her when she was older.

Jane stepped onto the escalator. How could she convince them that they must give her a dowry? How would she ever explain it in a way that would seem reasonable to them?

When her parents came out of customs, she ran to them, into her father's outstretched arms.

"Daddy, Mother, I am so happy you're here!" They kissed. Her father held her at arm's length to look at her. It felt so good to be with them again.

"I can tell you are in love," her father said.

"You look marvelous, darling," her mother said, kissing her again. "Your father and I are really very happy for you, now that we are over the shock of our little girl..." Her eyes filled with tears.

They went outside to the curb where Youssef was waiting for them in his Mercedes. Jane introduced them.

"*Mucho gusto en conocerlo,*" Youssef greeted them warmly.

"*Mucho gusto,*" responded her parents, surprising Jane. She asked them when they had learned Spanish. Her father winked at her.

"It happened since your phone call. Necessity, my dear."

She knew what a difficult prospect it was going to be for her parents to reconcile themselves to her getting married and living so far from them. However, she knew they loved her, and her happiness came before theirs.

They drove to the hotel, Youssef pointing out the sights along the way.

After her parents were settled in their rooms, they all went out to eat.

Youssef had made reservations at his favorite restaurant, El Cardenel. Mexican-style food, he explained, but no *arroz y frijoles*.

"This is the way rich Mexicans eat," he said.

Jane's father looked at Jane and raised his eyebrows. Jane ignored him, hoping Youssef did not notice. Youssef ordered the specialties of the house, starting with a delicious chicken meatball soup, followed by a Yucatan pork stew. They drank wine and they talked.

Jane's mother wanted to know about the family.

"So, Youssef, tell me about your sisters and brothers..."

Her father was interested in Youssef's business.

"Is it all right if I ask when your family business began? And who started it?"

Youssef was charming and Jane felt proud of him. Her parents seemed pleased. Youssef insisted on paying the check.

Youssef left Jane at the hotel with her parents. Once in their room, as she'd anticipated, her father asked,

"Okay, so what's this nonsense about a dowry?"

"Daddy, it's the custom here. It's the way young marrieds get started." Jane turned to her mother.

"I really hate asking you and Daddy to practically buy me a husband, but I have thought about it a great deal, and have to explain Youssef's family culture for you to understand. It's difficult, since first of all, his parents immigrated from Lebanon, a Middle Eastern culture, to Mexico, a more Western-type culture, but still different from American culture. I've spent a lot of time with his family and have gotten used to it. I've met quite a few young couples and talked about the dowry, and it seems that it is pretty normal in this Lebanese-Mexican society."

She paused and continued. "The fact is, there's simply no alternative. If I can't marry him, I will never marry."

"Now look here, Jane," said her father sternly. "Ask us for anything, and if it is at all possible we'll give it to you. You know that. But I object to your threat..."

"Oh, please Sam, don't start to lecture her," Jane's mother interrupted. "When Jane said that about not marrying, it was not a threat. I can see it in her eyes, how deeply she feels about Youssef. She loves him and wants to spend her life with him. Sam, you know how my Dad was against our marriage. What if I had listened to him?"

Her mother took Jane's hands into hers.

"I understand how you feel, darling. Your father," she turned and gave him a look, "will work something out about this dowry business. Now, we want to hear about Youssef's family, why they left Lebanon, and all about Mexico. We haven't really talked together for almost three months."

Jane told them how much more relaxed and unpressured life was in Mexico than in the States.

"My language classes at the University of the Americas helped me to get to know people. You know, Mom, all upper income people here have servants. There are so many native Indians who only work in houses as maids and cooks. I will have servants, too, after I'm married. You know, I told Youssef that I would be happy to go to work after we are married, and he really got upset. He told me women of our class do not work."

Sam laughed, "That's what I say, and we should not have given women the vote, either." Jane's mother shot him one of her looks.

Jane knew she could never explain some of Youssef's other ideas about how he expected her to behave. He did not want her to travel in the city buses — too common. She could not go to the open markets — those were for the Indian maids. And no housework — what would the maids do? Also, she needed to keep her eyes down when in a crowd, because men may think she was flirting, and he was jealous.

She enjoyed Youssef making the decisions about where or when they should eat or how they should spend the evening. With Youssef, those things were never left up to her. Ever since she was a small child her parents had made these same decisions for her, and now Youssef was taking over. She felt secure and taken care of.

Jane and her parents talked well into the night about her pending marriage, the dowry, and all the changes that were about to happen.

The next evening they went to Emir and Mariam Abboud's home for dinner. Youssef's parents gradually had accepted Jane with a slight reserve, but were quite charming to her mother and father. Emir and Mariam spoke English to them, and her parents tried in turn to speak a few words in Spanish. Jane introduced her parents to Youssef's nine brothers and sisters. Everyone was very polite, and she could tell how pleased her parents were with Youssef's family.

She was surprised when, after supper, the men went into Emir's study and closed the door. Her mother was obviously irked and tried to signal this to Jane, but Jane pretended not to notice because she knew no argument in her defense other than Youssef wanting it that way.

Jane and her mother and Youssef's sisters and his mother talked together, never mentioning the dowry, and when the men emerged, Jane noticed how pale her father was. Her mother and father exchanged looks.

"We're tired from our trip," her mother said, "and need a good night's sleep. We'll see everyone tomorrow."

Youssef and Jane dropped her parents at the hotel. Driving Jane home, Youssef told her angrily that he thought her parents were prejudiced against Lebanese, because of her father's negative attitude about the dowry.

"I will tell you again, Jane, I love you more than my life, but

I have my principles and my family customs, and under no circumstance will I give up what I rightfully deserve. It would be an insult to me as a man, as well as to my parents, to marry a woman with no dowry."

"I can't believe that if my parents refuse to give a dowry, you won't marry me."

"I am very sorry to have to answer you in this way, but yes, it would be impossible for us to marry. You will have to go back to your home with your parents. I will be deeply sad, but it can be no other way."

They arrived at her house and Youssef parked.

"Youssef, I missed my period and I took a pregnancy test this morning." She paused and then said quietly, "I'm going to have your child."

He was silent for a moment before saying, "Well then, under those circumstances, you have no choice. They must give you the dowry!" He reached across her and opened the door.

"Youssef," Jane started to say.

"Get out of the car, it's late," he said.

Jane stepped out of the car, and he drove away, leaving her standing in the street.

Jane telephoned her parents the moment she got into the house. Her father answered, and she told him that she wanted to come see them right away.

"Yes," he said, "we have some things to talk over with you as well."

Part VI

Her mother opened the door to the hotel room in her nightgown.

"Jane, darling, what's wrong? You look as though you've been crying."

Jane stood stiffly inside the door, unable to say what she knew she was going to have to say. Her father broke the silence.

"Jane, I don't like saying this to you now that you seem so upset, but this whole thing is ridiculous. You had better pack your things, and come home with us."

"What do you mean, Daddy?"

"Did you know they expect a dowry of one-hundred thousand dollars?"

Sweat broke out under her arms.

"We don't have that kind of money. And even if we did, I'd be damned before I would give it away like this. As far as I'm concerned, the idea of a dowry is absurd! We want you to get this whole thing out of your head!"

"Daddy, no." She began to cry again. She felt nearly hysterical. "You can bargain with them, explain to them, please, Daddy. I'm going to have Youssef's baby!"

"Oh, my God!"

"Jane," her mother said softly, "how could you be so foolish?"

Then nobody said anything. Her father sighed, very deeply.

"We agreed to meet with Youssef's parents tomorrow afternoon. I'll try to work something out." He kissed her.

"Don't worry sweetheart. Go home now. We all need some sleep."

Part VII

The two families met again at three o'clock the next day. The men went directly into the study and stayed there for several hours. Jane was annoyed with Youssef's mother. She seemed completely at ease, chattering on in mindless, mundane conversation, punctuated by the ringing of the small silver bell she kept next to her to call the maids.

Jane and her mother sat stiffly, anxiously waiting to see what was going to happen with the other meeting. Finally, the men appeared. Youssef was smiling. Her father asked if they could have dinner alone with their daughter that evening.

At dinner, her father told her that they had finally settled on a dowry of eighty-five thousand dollars. He told her they were going to sell some stocks they had and borrow the rest on his insurance.

"I want you to know that this is not easy on us. We are doing it because I don't have to tell you, you're everything to us."

Tears came to Jane's eyes. She felt so guilty for putting such a heavy burden on her parents.

"You can still change your mind, sweetheart," her father said. "You can always come back with us. There is still time to get your pregnancy taken care of. You know abortion is perfectly legal at home."

"Daddy, I love Youssef. I have never felt this way before. You know how much I love you and mom, yet because of Youssef, I am willing to come to a new country, be part of a different culture, make a complete change from the life I am familiar with. I want to be his wife. I want to have his child!"

"What about your education? Your new job?" asked her mother. "How can you live so far from us? When will we see you?"

"I don't care about the job. I love Youssef. That's the only thing that's important to me. We are only four hours apart by plane. I'll visit you often, and you can visit us, too."

"All right, Jane," her father said, taking her hand in his.

"You know that your happiness comes first for us. You are our only child, soon to be the mother of our first grandchild. Your happiness is worth far more than the money."

Jane and Youssef made plans for their wedding. It was to take place in three weeks.

Part VIII

Youssef and his family wanted the wedding to be in Mexico in a Muslim mosque, no less. It made sense, they said, since their family was the larger of the two, and since Jane and Youssef were to make their home in Mexico, that the wedding should take place there. Jane's parents objected at first, but when Emir insisted upon paying all the wedding expenses, they gave in. In addition to Jane's parents, her grandmother, two aunts, five cousins, and Susan were the only guests on the Baker side of the family.

Jane was sitting alone in her room waiting to be driven to the mosque when her father knocked and came into the room.

"Jane, I'm going to be candid with you."

Jane felt a twinge of fear, a feeling she'd had since she was a small child whenever her father confronted her. She watched him settle into an armchair.

"I deeply resent Youssef's family's take-over attitude," her father said, "their insistence on our giving an enormous cash wedding present to you" — he refused to use the term *dowry* — "and their insistence on the wedding being here, in a Muslim mosque. Sweetheart, you know you were raised Episcopalian. They simply have no regard for our wishes. It's outrageous."

"Daddy, we have been through all that, and you agreed on the dowry already."

"Oh, I'm totally aware of that. But look, sweetheart, there's still time for you to change your mind. I really don't know if we are doing you a favor by making this whole thing possible."

Jane opened her mouth, ready to speak, but her father put up his hand, indicating that he was not finished.

"You know that your mother and I have always given you everything you wanted. We may have over-protected and indulged you, I don't know. We haven't regretted it and I hope we never will."

"Daddy, you won't, I promise you. I feel really bad about your having to give Youssef so much money, but I know that after we are married and the baby comes, everything will be good again."

There was a knock at the door. "*Señorita, nos vamos en este momento.*"

It was time to go. Jane stood in front of the mirror and adjusted her ivory satin wedding dress. She turned and looked at her father and felt frightened. She knew what he'd said was true. The matter of the money was outrageous, and it disturbed her that Youssef had insisted upon it. She was beginning to feel that maybe her parents were right, and that this was really crazy. She quickly buried that feeling, though, because her baby must grow up with a father and she would allow nothing to dissuade her.

She walked slowly down the stairs and out to the Abbouds' limousine. The chauffeur drove her to the mosque. She felt anxious until she saw Youssef standing, tall and handsome, waiting for her.

Part IX

They went to Acapulco on their honeymoon. Jane loved being married. She adored having Youssef as her constant companion. His continual presence, his taking care of her, telling her when to wake, when to eat, what to wear, made her feel loved. It was easy, she didn't have to make any decisions, and she loved that. She put out of her mind the times he ignored her, asking her to leave the room when he was busy talking privately on his cell.

Her guilt about the dowry was diminishing and she looked forward to Youssef's lovemaking, sleeping in his arms at night, and waking with him in the morning. They ate when he wanted to eat, slept when he wanted to sleep, and talked together when he wanted to. She liked it that way, she felt as secure as she had as a child at home with her parents. She had no desire to be independent.

They had been in Acapulco for a week and were lying together on the beach, basking in the afternoon sun. She had not been feeling well due to her pregnancy. It was hot and she was feeling dizzy and nauseous.

"Youssef, I don't feel well, I'm going up to the room."

He appeared not to hear her. She repeated herself.

Again, he did not look up, but replied, "You will stay here with me."

"Youssef, really, I don't feel well. I have to go up and lie down."

She began to get up. Suddenly, she felt his hand on her arm, holding her tightly.

"Who are you going to meet in the room?"

She stared at him in disbelief. His handsome face was set and angry; she had not seen him this way since the night her parents came to Mexico and began talking about the dowry.

He kept a tight grip on her arm as he led her to their room. She was unable to speak, to answer his accusations.

"I saw you looking at him last night at dinner," he said angrily. "I suspected that you might try to meet him today!"

Jane was incredulous as she tried to remember what had happened last night at the restaurant. Suddenly she recalled whom he was talking about. The blonde American man, the one she thought she knew. She had stared at him, and he had returned her gaze.

They reached the room. Jane tried to explain, but Youssef would not listen to her. He opened the door and pushed her inside. He looked at her hard, then exited and closed the door. She heard him lock it and listened to his footsteps on the tile floor as he walked away.

She lay on the bed, feeling frightened by her new husband's behavior, not wanting to think of what it could mean. What could she do about his jealousy?

Part X

They returned to Mexico City. Youssef's parents had chosen an apartment for them in a recently completed building a block from their own apartment.

It was not that she did not like the apartment; she thought it was lovely, but she resented the fact that she and Youssef had not chosen it themselves. She knew this was the way things were done in his family, and she was afraid to bring the matter up to Youssef. She let it pass.

When the four of them went shopping to choose furniture, she felt as though she was just tagging along. When there was a choice to be made, like the color of a chair, it was made by Youssef and his parents. When she tried to express her opinion, Youssef told her to keep quiet.

"Are you pleased, *mi niña*, with your new furniture?" her father-in-law asked her unexpectedly, as they waited for the salesman to write up the order.

"Does it really matter if I am or not?" she answered dryly. She saw Emil's face darken. Youssef was standing across the room, inspecting their new purchases.

"Youssef," Emil nearly shouted, "*tu esposa* is rude and ill-mannered. *Yo salgo.*"

He turned and walked stiffly out of the store, his wife following, not looking at Jane.

Youssef came over to her, his face livid with rage. She felt frightened and sorry for what she had said.

"How dare you be rude to my parents?"

"I was not rude, I was only making a joke."

"You are lying. I believe my father before you. Go, get into the car!"

She waited for him, miserable and uncomprehending. He drove her home in silence.

When they got home he said, "Jane, you must honor my parents or God will punish you. Please write a letter to them and ask their forgiveness for your actions today."

Without really understanding why, but wanting to keep peace, she wrote the letter.

Two weeks later, two workmen appeared at the door to repair some faulty plumbing. She thought nothing of letting them in to accomplish their task.

When Youssef returned for the midday meal, she overheard the maids telling him about the workmen. She now knew that the maids watched her and reported to Youssef every day about her activities. When she looked at her husband as he came into the room, she knew he was in a rage again. Her heart sank.

"Did you make love with the workmen today, you whore?"

He continued berating her until she broke down in tears. He made her promise never to have a man in the apartment when he was not there. She would agree to anything if he would only be kind to her.

Every day, she learned something new about what Youssef expected of her. When they were together, she was not allowed to look at another man. When he thought she had, it would result in one of his rages, so she began to keep her eyes lowered almost all the time when they were together in public.

When she needed a new dress, she had to first tell Youssef, and then his parents would go shopping with them. He told her he did not trust her to shop alone, for her taste was too obviously American. He gave her only enough money each day for the maids to purchase food. She was not allowed any English reading matter.

He checked her computer to make sure her selected language was Spanish. He wanted her Spanish to improve, and instructed the maids to listen to her phone calls and to any visitors she may have and to let him know if they heard any English.

He allowed her no privacy, and kept the key to their mailbox so that he could read her mail. He checked her email daily, asking her, "Who is this?" And, "Is this a man or a woman?"

He spent very little time at home with no explanation as to where he was. One day, she felt so lonely that she called Susan, only to be told that she had returned to the U.S. a month earlier. Jane spent much of her time sleeping.

In spite of everything, she attempted to maintain a normal

exterior. Maria Teresa, her cook/housekeeper from Oaxaca, showed her the intricacies of mole sauce, and she also accompanied her on mushroom hunts in the various city parks. She really enjoyed these outings, feeling comforted in the quiet, mossy places under the giant trees. She loved the smell of the freshly picked mushrooms, and she began to learn which ones were tasty, which ones were not, which ones were dangerous, and which ones fatal.

In her e-mails and phone calls to her parents and American friends, she pretended her life was normal, like it had always been before her marriage.

With great effort, she behaved civilly to Youssef's family, who had been treating her coldly ever since the furniture store incident, despite the letter of contrition she'd sent them. She began to feel resentment toward them and to Youssef.

The adoration she had once felt for her husband was disappearing. Jane had gained weight and was feeling tired most of the time. She was lying on her bed one afternoon staring at the ceiling when the phone rang.

"*Bueno?*" she answered.

"Is this Youssef Abboud's wife?" said a man's voice with a distinctly American accent.

"This is *Señora Abboud.*"

"This is Victor Boswell. I'm calling to tell you to keep your husband home and away from my wife. Otherwise, he is going to get his lousy head blown off."

"Who are you?" she said, but he had hung up. She felt shocked and moved heavily off the bed. She stood in front of the mirror, repelled by how she looked. Her belly was distended in pregnancy, while her limbs and once beautiful face were pathetically thin. She was pale and had dark circles under her eyes. Her hair was a mass of tangled curls and needed brushing.

She sat in the living room, not moving, waiting for her husband to come home. The day had turned into evening when she finally heard Youssef's key turning in the lock. He switched on the lights and saw her sitting there.

"Don't you think you should be in bed, Jane? It is very late. You are not looking so good these days."

"Youssef, I want to leave you and go back home." The words began to spill out of her, uncontrollably.

"There was a phone call. I know you are seeing another woman. Please return my parent's dowry to me. I will also need my passport..."

His dark eyes narrowed. "What woman? And, what dowry?" he said, suddenly angry. "There is no woman and there is no more money! This apartment, this furniture," his arms made a sweeping gesture around the room. "Your clothes..."

"But what about your new business?"

"I have not had good luck in my business." He turned and began to walk out of the room. Jane moved heavily off the sofa, to follow him.

"Youssef," she began, "I cannot believe that all that money..."

He stopped, reached into his pocket, and dropped a bankbook on the floor in front of her. "Here, see for yourself."

He watched her as she bent over and picked it up. Indeed, the account had been closed. She was appalled. Eighty-five thousand dollars in seven months! She felt disoriented, ill, but somehow made her way to the bedroom. Later that night, she had her first labor pain.

Part XI

She was in the hospital. She could feel her baby move inside of her. Youssef's face came into focus, close to her own.

"The doctor says the baby is going to come soon. It is too early, the baby is premature, not quite seven months, but there is no control over such matters." He placed his hand on her belly and pressed down hard. Jane winced with pain.

"You have not been a good wife to me. God will punish you."

She screamed from the pain and the nurses came. They gave

her a shot, and she felt as though she were drifting on a calm sea. The softness was interrupted each time she had a pain. The pains became more frequent, causing her to cry out and beg for relief from those attending her. Each time she opened her eyes she saw Youssef.

The torturous hours passed slowly, the pains becoming more and more intense. She could feel the baby bearing down, as though the inside of her stomach was being pulled out from her.

She screamed, "I want to die, I want to die, kill me, kill me!" And then she felt a huge spasm totally out of her control, and then another, and another. Jane knew her baby was being born.

So convinced was she of the truth of Youssef's prophecy that she was afraid to look at her child for two days. She kept her eyes closed whenever they brought the baby to her.

Youssef told her they had named the baby Mariam.

"But Youssef," she protested, "you knew that I wanted to name her Rachel after my grandmother."

"The first-born child of the first-born son must always be named after his grandparents. It is our custom."

Her heart pounded with anger, but she said nothing. She needed time to rest and think.

Part XII

She completely understood now what Susan had tried to tell her months ago about how different Mexican men were from American men, how different the two cultures were.

She could no longer deny her reality. She could never adjust to this lifestyle; a mindless existence for a woman. She was repelled by her mother-in-law, and the way in which her days were spent at the hairdresser, shopping, or playing cards with her female friends. That was it; she made no decisions, was allowed no activity without her husband's consent. For Jane, raising her child in this culture was unthinkable.

The nightmare of the dowry was in the past. The money was gone and it was quite clear to her now that Youssef had never really loved her but rather had seen her as a type of interim financing, as if she were a bank. She rested over the next few days, and knew that she had to leave Youssef and Mexico and take her baby with her.

Now the door to her room opened, and in walked Youssef, smiling and looking happy.

"*Mi vida*, get dressed, you have been here five days, it is time to come home. You must recover quickly for we are going to make another baby right away. We are going to have lots of *niños* to make my parents happy. I just visited with little Mariam, and she is so beautiful. She makes me feel very proud."

He came near her, to embrace her. She shrank from him. The smile left his face and he took hold of her wrists, holding them so tightly that it hurt.

"You are insulting me when you act like this," he said. "You cannot refuse your husband something that is his right!"

"Youssef," she said almost inaudibly, "I don't love you anymore. As soon as I am strong enough, I am taking the baby and going home to California."

He struck her hard across the face. Shock washed over her.

"You have much to learn, Jane. When a woman is married in Mexico she belongs to her husband. She has no right to leave. You belong to me and I shall never let you go. My parents were correct. You are not a good wife for me. Still, we are married, and we shall remain married."

She stared at him and was silent.

"Should you have any ideas about running away, I will tell you now that it will be difficult but not impossible for you. However, you shall never take our child out of Mexico."

"What do you mean?" She was suddenly attentive.

He lit his cigarette deliberately, slowly, obviously enjoying the moment.

"In Mexico a birth must be registered after a child is born.

Without that registration, no passport or traveling papers can be issued. Because I do not trust you, I am not going to register our child." He watched her for a moment.

"Anything else you wish to know?"

She did not go home then as planned. Her doctor told them that she needed to remain in the hospital because of the apparent precariousness of her mental condition. She had no appetite and was losing weight. She could sleep only when given barbiturates. She felt sad, and when her doctor tried to impress upon her that she must get hold of herself, she could only nod, comprehending, but was unable to answer.

She was frightened by these feelings, but she did not wish to talk or think about anything but her baby. She longed to hold her and feed her, but the tiny baby had to remain in an incubator. Jane did not want to go home without her.

She lost track of time, the hours drifting into days. She was aware that she had to get away from Youssef somehow; the strong feelings of adoration she'd had for him had turned into feelings of disgust.

She needed to formulate a plan.

Her parents were coming to see the baby. She would tell them about her life with Youssef, how unhappy she was, and that she wanted to leave him. She would tell them about the difficulty with the baby's papers. Her father would know what to do.

Her energy returned, and her appetite improved. The prospect of being able to care for her baby soon, and of leaving Mexico with her parents, made her feel as though a weight had been lifted from her.

The phone rang. "Mother, I'm so happy you called!"

"We would have called sooner, dear, but Youssef told us you were in a depression, and that it would be better not to call for a time. Is the baby all right? We were told she is almost two months premature."

"Yes, she's fine. Perfectly formed, only very small. Just three pounds. She's in an incubator. I'm not allowed to care for her yet, but I see her every day."

"And you? Are you all right?"

"I was very depressed but I'm much better now, really fine, especially now when I hear your voice."

"Good, darling. I didn't want to tell you this until I was sure you were all right. Two weeks ago your father had a major coronary."

"Oh, no!"

"The doctors say he'll recover, but while his heart is mending, he must have complete rest. You know that we had planned to visit you and Mariam, but now the doctor does not want your father to travel for at least six months. He wants me to go without him, but I could never leave him at a time like this. You understand, darling, don't you?"

Part XIII

Jane awoke with a start; she had been dreaming that Youssef was dead. She lay quietly, still awash in the sensation of the dream, in the sudden sense of being free, released from the anguish she had been feeling for months. She relaxed in the comfort of knowing that it was in her power to be free. She only had to make a plan: Youssef had to die, then she could leave him.

The days passed, Jane grew stronger and returned home. Baby Mariam was still in the hospital and she and Youssef, always accompanied by her in-laws, visited her every day. It irritated her greatly when her mother-in-law would take the baby in her arms and walk away from Jane to where the chairs were arranged for visitors and sing songs in a language Jane did not recognize.

She thought, *Is this going to be my life?* And she always came up with the same answer: *No way!*

When baby Mariam was nearly two months old, they brought her home. Jane's days were filled with the feeding and care of her child, which made her happy. Now that she had her plan, she was able to tolerate Youssef. Her anger was offset by the knowledge that it was up to her to decide when it would be over.

Youssef noticed her changed attitude. "*Mi vida*, you have finally learned how to behave like a Mexican wife. I am so proud of you!"

When they began making love again, she took the birth control pills that she had secretly obtained from her female gynecologist, who understood and agreed with Jane that she needed more time before she had another child.

She e-mailed her parents every day, attaching photos of Mariam, and spoke with them once a week. Youssef continued working with his father at their company offices.

Often, she would push Mariam in her carriage over to her in-laws for lunch, Youssef and Emir coming home for the midday meal.

She learned to play cards with her mother-in-law and sisters-in-law, and went to the hair and nail salons with them. But her only interesting pastimes were cooking and mushroom hunting. Maria Teresa and she would come home with a full basket of mushrooms that Jane would prepare with Maria Teresa's help. Youssef seemed pleased. Not only was Jane now a good wife, she was also becoming an excellent cook.

She had told Youssef about her father's poor health and that it was not a good idea for her parents to travel. When Youssef was not enthusiastic about visiting her parents, she told him of her father's retirement from the insurance business and the sizable 401K funds that he wanted to invest, possibly in Youssef's latest business idea. Youssef immediately said that maybe it would be nice to see them in their home in San Diego after all.

They planned to visit her parents at Christmas. Youssef made all the arrangements, including plane tickets and passports. He applied for and received baby Mariam's birth papers. Jane placed the itinerary, visas, and birth papers in a folder in Youssef's desk. When she showed him how well organized it all was, he was very pleased.

During October, the weather was mild, and Jane and Maria Teresa went mushroom hunting two or three times a week. The wild mushrooms were in abundance. Their apartment was only two blocks from Chapultepec Park, the largest park Jane had ever been in. She loved walking through the lush subtropical gardens, wandering off the paths into more dense growth. She began to recognize the rich smell of damp earth, where they would find the mushrooms. Jane learned to prepare them in a variety of ways that Youssef enjoyed.

Before the end of the season, Jane slipped out of the house while Mariam was sleeping in the afternoon, went to one of their favorite hunting grounds, and picked four of the mushrooms Maria Teresa had pointed out as among the most poisonous of them all, the *Amanitia Phalloides*. She'd told her that once eaten, flu-like symptoms did not appear immediately, but did so after a day or two. Then the illness would continue, sometimes for as long as a week before the person died from what was often diagnosed as a severe form of flu.

Jane placed the mushrooms in a paper bag and hid them on the top shelf of her closet, behind two large hatboxes. She inspected them weekly. They were drying nicely.

Finally, it was December. The date of their departure was three days away. She waited for the maids to go to their rooms after lunch, took the bag of dried mushrooms off the shelf in her closet, ground them into a powder in the coffee grinder, and transferred the powder to a small glass bowl, which she placed on the spice shelf. She wrapped the grinder in plastic, went out of the apartment and discarded it, along with the paper bag that had held the mushrooms, in the neighbor's *basura*, two blocks from their apartment. That same day, she purchased a new grinder, the same color and brand as the one she had just thrown away.

That afternoon, she spent time helping Maria Teresa make

Youssef's favorite dish, *frijoles con tomates, ongos y chiles,* adding the mushroom powder from the glass bowl along with the fresh mushrooms and chiles. She warned the maids not to eat any of this dish, as Youssef wanted it for lunch the next day.

That evening at dinner, Youssef enthusiastically ate the *frijoles con tomates, ongos y chiles* she had prepared for him. When he asked her why she was only eating soup and not the *frijoles,* she told him her stomach had been upset that day and thought beans were not the best thing for her. He ate everything on his plate.

After dinner, when the dishes had been cleaned and put away, she paid the maids, gave them all a Christmas bonus, and told them they could go home tomorrow after lunch and that she would see them on the fifth of January when she, Mariam, and Youssef returned from California.

The next day, when Youssef came home for lunch, he said he was not feeling well, and wanted to lie down. Jane saw that he was very pale, and he soon said he felt nauseous. He vomited and complained of diarrhea and terrible stomach cramps. By the evening, his symptoms had intensified, and Jane told him she was worried and called an ambulance.

They went to the emergency room and Youssef was diagnosed with severe gastroenteritis. He was given medications and sent home.

He slept most of the next day, but when his symptoms didn't diminish, Jane lied to him and said she was canceling the trip and was going to call the doctor. Youssef, pale and weak, smiled at her and told her how wonderful she was. She came back shortly, and, lying once again, told Youssef that she had spoken to the doctor who'd said it could take a week for him to begin to feel better and that he should take his medicine and rest. She gave him more of the medication prescribed by the doctor. She left the room and closed the door softly.

She walked down the hall into the entryway and looked into the living room. She hated the furniture and the religious

Muslim art on the walls. She felt excited, grown up, finally, to be leaving this unhappy place, never to return.

The phone ringing interrupted her thoughts. She hesitated, went to the phone, and decided not to answer it. It rang several more times, then went to voice mail. She turned up the volume and heard her mother-in-law asking about Youssef and how was he feeling and did he need anything.

"Call me back and let me know." *Click.*

Jane stood there for a moment, enjoying the knowledge that she was leaving.

She walked to the hall closet where she had placed her suitcase. Then she went to Youssef's desk, and removed the folder with her plane ticket, visa, and birth papers. She went into Mariam's room and stood next to her crib. She changed her diaper. While the baby was on her back, Jane played with her, making her laugh, the cute deep gurgling sound Jane loved so much.

She picked Mariam up, placed her in her Snugli carrier, and adjusted the straps until it felt comfortable. Jane loved carrying her baby like this. She walked into the hallway where she picked up her suitcase and travel bag. She opened the front door, looked back briefly over her shoulder, stepped out into the hallway, and closed the door gently behind her.

CPSIA information can be obtained
at www.ICGtesting.com
Printed in the USA
FSHW011703070220
66829FS